MW01241579

Novels
The Lords of Xibalba
The Oil Eater
Blocking Paris
Edge of the Pit
The Catalina Cabal
Exodus from Orion
Quick Read
Legend of the Broken Paddle
Poets and Philosophers
The Island Classic

Novellas
A Present for Kainani

Middle Grade Books
Hunt for the Wild Honu
Hunt for the Wild Taro
Hunt for the Wild Pueo

A Present for Kainani

A Christmas Novella

Bill Thesken

KOLOA PUBLISHING

Paperback ISBN 978-1-7372521-6-0
Hardcover ISBN 978-1-7372521-8-4
E-Book ISBN 978-1-7372521-7-7

1.

Twas the morning after Christmas and per the house laws, not a creature was stirring, not even Santa Claus.

But even though the big guy was not stirring, and lay still as a log, his breathing was labored.

The transfer of air from nostrils to lungs and then back again like two enormous armies that were warring, and it soon became apparent that the large man was absolutely, and most decidedly snoring.

Mrs. Claus had enough, and even though she was not in charge of that tremendous task of delivering all the presents on Christmas Eve, she certainly had her hands full throughout the entire year keeping a giant house full of elvish toymakers happy and fed. She cooked and cleaned, organized, and mended, kneaded and prodded and coaxed, tended to every need and want, for churning out toys for every good girl and boy in the world was not only a chore, it was a team effort. She looked forward to this day off just as much as everyone else did.

She opened her eyes ever so slightly at the tumultuous bellowing of air, and poked Santa ever so gently on the shoulder, hoping he would turn over and stop snoring.

"What? What happened?" he blurted out, rudely awaked from his gentle dream of rolling meadows filled with bright yellow and blue flowers.

"You were snoring," she said simply and rolled over facing away.

Santa's eyes fluttered then opened, his visions of warm green grass and blue skies still filling his mind's eye. He opened the curtain next to the bed, and outside all was white snow and black sky filled with stars and half a moon setting in the west, and that made him smile.

They were safe at home at the North Pole.

He looked over at Mrs. Claus, her back turned to him, thick blanket tucked over her head and patted her gently on the shoulder, then sat up on the other side of the bed and wriggled his toes deep in socks on the cold hard floor.

"Brrr," he whispered to himself and arose slowly, his beard pushing off his chest as he stood seemingly leveraging his large frame off the bed, bones creaking, suddenly searching for warmth after being tucked in the comfy bed he went to the nightstand and slipped on thick flannel pants and jacket, closed the door behind him as he made his way down the hall to the bathroom and smiled at himself in the mirror, giant white beard flowing from ear to ear down to the middle of his chest, and white hair from the top of his head, long curly locks draping clear over the edge of his collar, and got to work. It was the day after Christmas, and the beginning anew. With scissor and razor, he chopped and then shaved every single follicle from his face till it was smooth and gleaming pure white as the hair still remaining on the top of his head and then he got to work on that.

Within a half hour all the white hair was gone, and from the top of his head to the tip of chin, all was bare like the skin of baby's bun and he managed a grin.

"Let the new year start," he whispered knowingly. For it was true, the new year for Santa and the elves began the day *after* Christmas.

"Let it begin," he whispered.

The blizzard of hair on the floor wasn't silver with age, it was pure white like the snow that enveloped the land, a genetic disposition.

Throughout the year from this first day forward, his hair would grow again full and bushy like a giant tree, his head like a farm of fertile ground and roots.

One joke that ran through the legion of elves whose chins were perpetually bare, was that Santa was a hair farmer.

He studied his face in the mirror for a moment not more. Some wrinkles were starting to appear at the edges of his eyes, from squinting most likely. Just entering his early forties, more wrinkles were sure to appear as time marched on. His father, Santa Claus the ninth rest his soul lived to a hundred and one, and with good luck he, Santa Claus the tenth would last at least as long.

Someday, hopefully soon there would be a Santa Claus the eleventh running barefoot around the house, but for now the cupboard was bare so to speak, the crib in the children's room was empty, and Mrs. Claus was silent on the subject.

He tiptoed down the stairs to the main living area, the great room in the middle, the kitchen on the side and the row upon row of big rooms with all the doors open full of small slumbering shapes.

The elves would be sleeping, most of them, all throughout the day, with just a few rustlings about in the big house next to the toy factory, for as it was with all companies big and small and families of people for that matter, some were not built for slumber or vacationing or relaxing at all, for some it was calming to be at work, and to be without a task at hand, no mission to accomplish, no duty to fulfil, was itself like tedious work or worse, a slow agony, a torture to be idle, and some of them would be tinkering and playing and planning for the coming year.

Santa visited the reindeer.in the big barn They were all wiped out. Wouldn't you be after flying around the world pulling a giant sleigh with the big guy and enough toys for every good girl and boy, and were busy now laying in piles of hay. Rudolph's nose was black as a lump of coal fresh from the mine, even though the night before they relied on its red glow to make their way through the foggy night, especially around London town.

He checked the sleigh. A couple of bolts loose, nothing missing. It would get a thorough tune-up and flight test before next year.

They only had a couple of rough landings on the long trip around the world, one on the outskirts of Oldenburg, Germany just south of the icy North Sea, and the other in Paramus New Jersey, just about twenty miles north of New York City. The bright lights of the big city and the driving snow and darkness after they headed north over the Big Apple messed with the reindeer's eyesight, and even Rudolph's bright shiny nose couldn't help them with the rocky road next to the orphanage.

The left sled was bent in the middle from a boulder the size of a bowling ball that was hidden in the snow. Santa crouched low and ran his finger over the angled iron sled that would need to be straightened with a hot torch and hammer, and that's when he noticed a little bit of gold ribbon sticking out from underneath the back of the sled.

"Well now," he muttered, "what is this?"

He pulled at the edge of the ribbon, hoping that was all there was, just a bit of gold tinsel, and nothing more, but as he pulled and pulled, the ribbon kept coming, unwinding from some source under the carriage and then it stopped, stuck on something and he gave it a quick tug, and that something came loose, and that something that came loose was a golden wrapped present the size of a loaf of bread.

Santa's breath was stuck in the back of his throat as he witnessed the package settle gently into the straw on the floor, and then he sighed gently, and disappointedly.

It was a present.

He picked it up, nestled the glasses on the edge of his nose and read the inscription.

To: Kainani

From: Santa

Santa cursed gently under his breath, the vilest curse that could only venture forth from his lips in time of utter and dire distress:

"Confound it."

He shook his head and thought hard. There were nine bags of presents on the sled, one for each of the seven continents, then one for the islands in the Caribbean, and one for the islands in the Pacific. This present must have bounced free of the bag when they landed hard in either Oldenburg or Paramus, and probably came from the Pacific Islands bag that was on this side of the sled and packed towards the back:

For Kainani was a Polynesian name.

Santa picked up the present and sighed mightily again while walking back to the great house, snow crunching under his feet. One of the elves saw him and began to wave and smile, but then saw what he was carrying, and his smile turned into a worried frown. There weren't supposed to be any leftovers, not when it came to presents.

This was serious business.

Santa stared down at the present, wrapped tightly in gold reflecting paper, about the size of a shoe box, he shook the box gently. It sounded like shoes, there was one way to find out but he daren't open the present to check, as it was bad luck to open a present that was not meant for you. He sighed and shook his head.

One way indeed, and one way only. He headed for his office on the side of the workshop, turned on the lights and there on the desk wrapped in a ribbon, ready to be filed away with all the other books from years past was the book of wishes.

"Not yet," he whispered to the tightly bound book. "Not just yet for you to be filed away. There is work still to do."

He unraveled the ribbon and opened the heavy front cover, then put his finger on the tab that read 'K', leafing through the names. There were quite a few names that started with K, many more with Ka, and lot with Kai: Kaikea, Kailani, Kaimana, and there it was at long last, Kainani, age seven who wanted a pair of light and airy running shoes, the kind that made it seem as though you were wearing a pair of clouds, size nine.

"Size nine?" Santa remarked. "She must be a big girl for shoes like that." He remarked most innocently since it mattered to him not one bit the size or shape of a child, since it was the size and shape of their heart that mattered the most. And if Kainani was on the list, then she must have a heart the size and shape that was necessary to have her wish relayed to the list. It was a strange and ancient rule, and even though Santa himself didn't quite understand or know exactly how it worked, somehow it just did.

He ran his finger along and across the line to the address, twenty-two fifty-three Kapahulu Avenue, Honolulu, Hawaii.

There was no choice to made. No alternative, or decision that needed reflection or advice. The only option was clear and true. They would have to make a road trip, or in this case, heading to the Hawaiian Islands, a sky trip.

On a commercial airliner, on the carrier's terms and conditions.

Unfortunately for Santa, and Mrs. Claus for that matter as well, the magic of Christmas as far as their travel was concerned, only lasted for one sweet night.

What was first class accommodations on Christmas Eve, a plush silk lined sleigh and eight magic reindeer at your beck and command, travel anywhere in the world and all over the world, was coach on all the other days of the year, and leave the flying to them. Take it or leave it pal.

2.

Booking a last-minute flight to Hawaii from any location in the world is a trick in itself.

Booking it last minute the day after Christmas in the middle of the coldest winter in recent memory at an airport in Alaska full of grumpy half frozen popsicle people who can't wait to get out of the perpetually dark ice rink blizzard, and into the balmy palm tree lined, white sand rimmed trade wind brushed baby blue waters of Waikiki wouldn't be a trick, it would be a miracle.

The woman behind the counter was pleasant and calm. Her demeanor perfectly suited to dealing with an unruly mob that could at any moment in time tear her to bits and pieces like a pack of wolves. The only thing separating her from disaster was the stainless-steel counter in front of her, the confident look in her eyes, and the demure set of her jaw, lips not smiling, and not frowning, positive, self-assured, all business. This wasn't her first rodeo. One sign of weakness and it was all over.

"I'm sorry Mr. Claussen, the best we can do is put you on stand-by for our midnight flight."

Santa smiled, the edges of his eyes twinkling as he poked Mrs. Claus on the hip.

"Well momma, it's the best we can do. We'll take it," he said cheerily and passed the credit card across the counter to her.

Christopher Claussen was the name on the card and it wasn't an alias. Somehow along the line, many years ago when they were first starting out, the Claussen family name as far as Chris was concerned anyways, was shortened to Claus by mistake. One of the chroniclers of his family's initial fame in doing good deeds, way back in the 16th century mis-spelled the name, and rather than confuse people, his ancestors and namesakes decided to just 'go with it' as far as the public was concerned, but for sake of their family heritage, they would keep the Claussen name for official business.

Some other people thought Santa's real name was Kris Kringle, but that was another misnomer that could be blamed on his preference of a certain snack cake by that very name.

And so, the time came when the ticketed passengers boarded, row after row after row.

Time ticked away as errant ticket holders were summoned, and slowly the waiting area at the gate emptied out leaving two.

"Mr. and Mrs. Claussen, please come to the boarding gate," said the voice on the intercom, even though they were sitting right there next to the gate in full view of the announcer.

As they finally entered the door of the plane everyone stared in dismay at the large man walking down the aisle. How in world was he going to fit in any of the seats? Surely, he needed an entire row to himself. Couldn't they fit him up front in first class? Or maybe they were going to sit him down in the middle of the aisle at the back of the plane, like ballast on a boat, you couldn't put him on one side or the other or the plane would tip over mid-air.

He smiled as he went with Mrs. Claus trailing behind him. She was also smiling; they were after all going to Hawaii. The plane seemed to adjust as he walked, or was that just the bags being loaded down below in the luggage bays? Not it couldn't be, those trucks had departed long ago and the hatches secured.

There were two seats left, way at the back, almost there. Both passengers sitting next to the empty seats gulped in fear, both were on the aisle just opposite the bathroom door, one with a middle-aged lady who looked about anxiously to see where the big man was headed.

Santa smiled down at her as he stood in the aisle next to the empty seat. The woman grinned sheepishly as Santa gestured to his wife behind him and said simply: "You should sit here Momma."

In the next row was the last remaining seat on the entire plane and all eyes from front to back were watching and waiting for the outcome. Even the people up in first class were leaning out into the aisles and standing with their heads up against the bulwarks, craning their necks to get a glimpse of the action. What would happen? You could cut the thick tension in the air with a butterknife.

Santa smiled at the man sitting in the middle seat who reluctantly and glumly realized that he was the lucky recipient of the last guest on-board. He slid his forearm off the arm rest in between the seats realizing that it's use as far as he was concerned was as good as gone for the entire flight, then gestured bravely, and mightily to the empty cushion beside him.

On the other side of this heroic man, in the window seat sat a young man of about five or six who, if it could be believed, was even more valiant than his father. He tugged on his father's arm to bring him closer and whispered in his ear:

"I'll sit in the middle poppa."

The switch was made not quickly, but deliberately and the young lad sat in the middle seat looking up with awe at what he knew should be, could be, must be...

He almost couldn't bear the thought, because at his young age he still believed, but how in the world could it be possible that Santa Claus could be on the same plane, and sitting right next to him?

The very thought that it was impossible faded quickly as the large man reached into his side pocket and pulled out a toy airplane the size of his fist and handed it to him. It was a miniature jet airplane with one engine on each side of the wings that glowed orange in front and blew air out the back, the cockpit and fuselage were lit a crisp greenish white, he could see the pilots hard at work in the front, and all the passengers and even the stewards and stewardesses all the way towards the back.

He squinted his eyes at the last row of seats, peering with one eye into the window, and there was a tiny model of a young boy with brown hair just like him, a dad in the window seat, and if he tilted the window just right, there on the end seat was a big man dressed in a red suit with red hat and a big white beard.

He gasped quickly in wonder and looked up quickly at the big man sitting next to him, though not wearing a red suit and red hat, and even though he had no big white beard, there was a twinkle in his eye, and he winked down at the young boy who promised silently to himself that this was going to the best airplane ride in history, and next Christmas was going to be a bonanza of presents under the tree if he played his cards right.

3.

"Now remember Santa whispered to Mrs. Claus as they got off the plane. "Here in Hawaii, we're Mr. and Mrs. Claussen, Chris and Melissa. Ix-nay on the Santa Claus-ay," he admonished her in pig Latin.

Down in Waikiki, the taxi turned off the main strip and drove down a wide boulevard lined with palm trees and finely trimmed bougainvillea hedges, wide sidewalks teeming with happy tourists of all shapes and sizes and stopped at the entrance to the Royal Hawaiian Hotel. There was a wide red carpet that ran all the way from the taxi door to the front desk hidden somewhere deep inside the hotel

The doorman beamed as he greeted them, each with a lei, one for Melissa and one for himself. The bellman grunted as he lifted the giant suitcase out of the trunk. Chris paid the driver the fare plus a ten spot for good service.

He handed the doorman another ten spot for the fine greeting and leis, and the bellhop another ten for nearly breaking his back. They didn't travel first class very often, but when they did, Chris knew what to do.

They walked slowly down the red carpet, Chris could sense the delight in Melissa, the air was balmy and warm, the trade winds blowing gently through the lobby towards the blue ocean that they could see up ahead.

Melissa browsed in the gift shop while Chris checked in. She wanted to spy on the competition to see what was new and decided to pick up a couple of books to read by the pool.

Up in the room on the second floor with a balcony that looked over the pool towards the ocean Chris tipped the bellhop that brought their giant bag since he was a different one that took it out of the taxi.

He looked at the bag from the gift shop that Melissa set down on the desk and pulled out three thick paperback books. Not your typical studious reading material, the covers had elegant women and dashing men in provocative poses next to sunsets and mansions.

"Are these romance novels?" he asked.

"They're books," she replied simply.

"So, you think you're going to just sit by the pool and read trashy romance novels all day? You realize this is a working vacation, we have a job to do."

She smiled as she plucked the book out of his hand and laid it back on the desk.

"Maybe for you it's a working vacation. For me it's just a vacation." She poked him gently on the tip of his nose while he grunted and threw her hair back haughtily and went back out onto the balcony to take in the scene which was quite spectacular. Fluffy white clouds filled a velvet blue sky over an impossibly aqua blue ocean, gentle white foamed waves rolling in from up and down the coast, surfers and canoes, swimmers, floaties and boats, the jagged edge of diamond head jutting out into the action, and the pool surrounded by umbrellas, cocktail waiters and waitresses floating around and through the edges, the soft smoke from a barbecue at the poolside restaurant filling the air with aroma.

Chris for his part, emptied his pockets, and remembering one especially important piece of paper, retrieved it from his front shirt pocket. It was a wish list of all the toys the young lad sitting next to him on the plane wished that he could have, and the list seemed to encompass just about every toy that was ever made in the history of the world, it was after all a long flight and there was plenty of time to be thorough after all.

He plopped the big suitcase on the bed, cracked it open with a pop and there nestled safely in the middle cushioned by soft socks and shirts was the rascal present that necessitated this trip in the first place. The gold wrapped box with size nine shoes for a young Hawaiian girl named Kainani, and the second time in the past few days that it had been in this general location.

Chris looked at Melissa on the balcony, blissfully enraptured by the view, and sighed. A working vacation indeed.

"I'll be back soon!" he shouted, then pulled

out a small red sack, a miniature model from the one used on Christmas Eve, stuffed the gold present inside, picked up a plastic key card from the desk and headed out the door.

4.

Deciding to walk since he was a little out of shape nearly turned into a disaster. Straight off the plane from Alaska where it was five degrees above zero to a blazing Hawaiian sun eighty-five degrees in the shade and what seemed like a million in the sun was a bit too much of a change for the big guy. His cheeks a ruddy red, sweat beading on every inch of lily-white skin he trudged on through the hotel filled concrete jungle towards Kapahulu Avenue which with every step seemed to be located on the opposite side of the planet.

Since the gravity near the equator was less than at the North Pole, Chris actually weighed less. The earth was not actually a perfectly round sphere but an oblate spheroid with a diameter at the equator nearly twenty-seven miles larger than at the poles.

Centrifugal force spinning as it was like a pizza pie thrown in the air compressed at the top edges, the poles were closer to the center where the gravity was gathered, the edges of the equator farther away, not by much, but it could be measured, and it amounted to approximately one percent difference in weight. A three-hundred-pound man at the North Pole would weigh two ninety-seven at the equator. Three pounds difference. It wasn't however, enough to matter for poor old Chris.

He stopped at three different convenience stores for cold bottled water, and at the last one decided to splurge on a mango soda.

He stopped walking again next to a bus stop with two benches and a shady tree that was big enough for both. There was a round hole in the sidewalk in between the benches and tree grew right out of the center and Chris marveled at the sight, either they had drilled a big hole and planted the tree in the center, or the tree was already growing and they poured the concrete around it.

While Chris took up residence on one of the benches, on the other sat an elderly man leaning on a cane with black hair streaked with silver, and skin brown and taught.

"How are you doing sir?" asked Chris politely.

The other man smiled with a twinkle in his eye. It had been a boring morning so far with no one to talk with. He was on his way to the checkerboards down in Waikiki to make battle with some of the other crusty old-timers and needed to brush up on his verbal combat skills when luck would have it, a haole fresh off the boat sat down right next to him. He decided to have a little fun.

"Howzit haole."

Chris squinted his eyes, and tilted his head,

rolling the words around in his ears to keep them in play till he could figure out what was just said.

"What?"

The man just smiled back at him and Chris wondered if he spoke English or some other language. Maybe the old man was greeting him in Hawaiian. He mouthed the words twice, slowly just as he heard them.

"How-zit-how-lee. Is that how you say hello in Hawaiian?" asked Chris.

The old man chuckled.

"That's how we say hello to someone who looks like you."

Chris looked down at his stomach.

"No, not because you're fat."

"Be nice."

"Okay, okay. It's not because you're... how do we say... well rounded...it's because you're white."

Chris sighed, and the old man could see the genuine disappointment in his eyes.

"So, you're a racist."

"Not me brah. I'm just telling you like it is."

"Yeah right."

"Hey sometimes we begin the sentence with damn haole or effin' haole. You're getting off easy today."

"Whatever," said Chris as he took a deep breath and got ready to start walking again. He just needed another couple of minutes in the shade, and then he'd get going once more.

The old man recognized the kindness in Chris's eyes and decided to give him a break and make amends. Plus, he could see the guy was getting ready to leave and he needed someone to talk with until the bus got there.

"Eh brah, it's not a big deal, believe me. You see the word haole is Hawaiian. It literally means without breath. Back in the old days the Hawaiian's used to greet each other by breathing close and right into each other noses. When the first white men came to the islands, they did not share that custom, in fact they abhorred it, they refused to do it, and so the term 'haole', was used to describe them. The correct pronunciation is 'hah-ole' like you're laughing and fighting a bull, but we just say how-lee."

"Sounds Chinese."

"It's Hawaiian. Take my word for it."

"So, I'm a haole?"

The old man shrugged his shoulders.

"Don't take it so hard buddy."

"Why's that?"

"I'm hapa."

"What's that?"

"Hapa means half. I'm half haole. My last name's Alexander."

Chris slapped his thigh and laughed.

"Don't let it go to your head haole. I'm hapa, one step up. You're still full haole."

"So, you get to tell me what to do?"

"I get to tell what *for* do. Use proper pidgin."

"That's no fair."

"Aren't you fresh off the boat?"

"We took a plane."

"Where you from?"

Chris told the truth.

"North Pole."

Now it was the old man's turn to squint, and he slapped his thigh in appreciation. "Good one. I gotta use that on old Chumlee today. I'll ask him if he's from the North Pole bearing gifts for me. We play checkers, quarter a game. It's good fun."

"I'm Chris."

"I'm Kaipo. My friends call me Kolohe, that means rascal in Hawaiian."

"I can see why."

A tall slender man walked by with a small brown dog on a leash. The man himself looked rich, with new white tennis shoes, navy blue crisp ironed shorts, polo shirt, gold watch.

"Howzit haole," said Chris as he passed.

The man looked at him with a frown, shook his head while muttering under his breath, and kept walking.

"What? What bodda you?" said the old man at the back of retreating man's head, eyes boiling with mock rage.

"Bodda you?" asked Chris, puzzled.

"What, you no speak pidgin eh howl-lee? Dats okay, I teach you." He pointed across the street at another old guy who gave him the finger. "You see dat kine buggah ovah dare? He no can, always get one attitude, one mana'o."

The old man shouted across the street.

"Eh, you get one pilikia? You get one problem? Get one job! Ha, ha,ha!"

The other man looked over and laughed back mockingly.

"What? Bodda you?"

Chris took note. 'What?', and 'bodda you?' seemed to be two very important phrases that were used quite often for greeting here in the islands.

The old man sitting next to him replied.

"Eh, you no can, what brah you like beef, you like trow?"

"Bumbye!" the other man shouted with a laugh. "You da one going have pilikia!" Then limped away on his cane.

Two old men in their seventies yelling across a busy street at each other for fun. Chris shook his head.

Now Santa Claus / Chris could understand every language in the world, it was his job after all to be able to decipher any words, and most times it was easy since in many ways all languages were the same and had a common root, but pidgin was not a language. It was a mish mash polyglot take half a phrase or syllable from one language, smash it into another, roll it into a third and throw it into the air.

All he needed was a Rosetta stone.

"Can you teach me pidgin?"

"Right now? Brah, it takes years. Besides, here comes my bus, unless you like ride with me to Waikiki?" He asked hopefully. He was beginning to enjoy Chris' company.

"No, I have to walk to Kapahulu. Maybe we can meet up some other time. Just a couple of phrases, and I'll figure it out."

"Okay, I'll give you a quick tip. If someone

asks if you 'like beef', or 'like trow' you say no, because those mean to fight, okay?"

"What about bumbye? That's what your friend told you."

"That means later on, by and by, some other time. Don't say that either unless you're friends."

The bus slowed down and began to pull over to the curb. The old man got slowly to his feet leaning on his cane.

"Check you later," he said.

"Bumbye," said Chris.

That brought a smile to the old man's face.

"One last thing you gotta know bruddah, before we part ways."

"What's that?"

"Howzit, bumbye, and the handshake. Very important. Three parts of aloha. If you got this down, you're in there."

The old man reached out his right hand, grabbing Chris's hand thumbs interlocking, then unclasped, slid down into a normal handshake, then slid quickly backwards till just the tips of the fingers were locked, then released.

"That's the bruddah bruddah Hawaiian style handshake."

"So, this took the place of the nose breathe greeting," said Chris matter of factly.

The old man grinned. "Now you're getting it cuz. Pretty soon you'll be a real kanaka, a true Hawaiian."

The bus shut its doors and roared off in a cloud of dust.

With reluctance Chris got to his feet and continued on with his journey.

With a little huffing and puffing and superhuman effort aided by a precise GPS location from his nifty elf made watch, in less than half an hour he was standing in front of 2253 Kapahulu Avenue, and the last loose thread of the year was ready to be mended.

It was a simple house with a flower garden in pots by the front door. On the side of the house stood a row of surfboards lining against the wall and stretching towards the back. With miniature red sack over his shoulder, he walked up the stairs. There would be no magical entry through a keyhole or down a chimney today. For some strange reason that magic only worked on Christmas Eve, and no other time.

Circumstances as they were, this present would have to be delivered in person.

Just as he was about to knock on the door a tiny voice came from the side, from the neighbor's porch where sat an old oriental woman on a rocking chair: "They're not home."

Dang thought Chris.

"Are they at work?" he asked hopefully. "They'll be back later tonight?"

She shook her head. "They're gone for the week."

Chris's heart sank. He walked slowly over to the old woman's porch so he could talk with her.

"I have a package to deliver."

"Are you with the post office?"

"No, private delivery system."

"You could leave it with me and I can give it to them when they get back."

He thought for a moment shook his head.

"No, that won't work."

He wouldn't be able to rest without knowing for certain that the gift was delivered and so it would have to be delivered in person, nothing less.

The old woman shrugged her shoulders.

"Do you know where they went by chance," he asked hopefully. Please don't say Alaska, he prayed silently.

"Well, not exactly. I sort of know that they travel around the islands visiting with their family. It's a tradition for them and they do it every year. I'm sorry I don't' know."

She shook her head for a moment, then suddenly perked up and snapped her old fingers as a brilliant thought came to her mind.

"I've got an idea who might know where they went. The mother works at a hotel in Waikiki...." Her voice faded as she gazed into the distance, "but I don't know which one, they're so many and they all seem the same..."

Then she perked up again: "But the father works as a beach boy in front of Duke Kahanamoku's statue right there in the center of Waikiki. He rents out surfboards and gives surfing lessons and canoe rides. All those boys, they all know each other, and sometimes they come over here to the house after work and play the ukulele and have barbecues. They're kind of a wild bunch. Go ask the beach boys down at Waikiki. One of them will know where to find them."

Chris smiled, reached into his pocket, and pulled out a ten-dollar casino chip from Vegas and handed it to her.

Her eyes lit up at the sight of it. "What's this for?"

"For helping me."

She scoffed and held it back out towards him.

"You don't have to pay me for that."

"It's okay, I have no use for it, I never go to Vegas."

"Well, how do you know that I go there"

He smiled and winked at her knowingly, and she winked right back with a big grin.

"You rascal haole man, how'd you know, I'm going next week."

She pinched the coin tightly and motioned towards the miniature sack over his shoulder.

"And I'll put it on red."

5.

Chris walked halfway back to the hotel and called it quits, waved down a cab and rode the rest of the way.

H searched for Melissa in the hotel, up in the room it was quiet and cool. He looked longingly at the freshly made bed, the cover tight, yet soft, and thought about taking a nap, then winced.

Not a chance.

He placed the little sack on the desk and went out the door, down the elevator and made his way to the pool. He knew where she'd be.

In a little cabana in the shade, he found her. Big sunglasses, big hat, cool drink on the little table next to the lounge chair, feet propped on a little pillow, book wide open intensely reading, pages turning.

Next to the cool drink on the table was a half-eaten fish sandwich smothered with pickles, and the remnants of a hot fudge sundae. Melissa was in full vacay mode.

She saw him over the edge of the book and gave him the thumbs up.

He returned a thumbs down.

"She wasn't home. This might take longer that I thought."

Melissa, however, did not seem overly disappointed. In fact, Chris thought he detected a little wrinkle of a smile on the edge of her lips, and if he could only see through the dark sunglasses, perhaps a glint of happiness in her eyes.

He feinted a frown and huffed.

"Yes, well it looks like we'll need to stay a bit longer I'm afraid."

"Oh, that's too bad," she said drawing out bad till it was almost a different word.

"Why don't you have a sit and rest for a while. You look a little tired, and your skin is turning red."

"Not just yet."

All business again.

"I must visit the beach boys to find our Mr. Bull Kaupea. It seems that he's taken his family on a traditional trip around the islands."

"The beach boys?"

"Not the band. Probably who that band was named after though. They work on the beach renting surfboards and canoes; they sound like a very hearty crew. Full of life and good cheer. Would you like to come with?"

She smiled sweetly. "No thank you, I'm comfy right here." She reached in her big bag next to the chair and handed a tube of sunscreen to him. "Now you put this on right now mister. No ifs ands or buts."

He complied, in the shade of the cabana, took off his hat, squeezed a big lump of white goo in his hand and lathered it on top of his stubbly head, neck and ears, nose and big cheeks, that were, like the top of head beginning to stubble up with new white hair, then up and down arms and legs.

"Happy now?" he asked her.

She answered. "Quite."

"Well, I'm off now," he announced as he put the hat back on his head, expecting a grand send off.

"Have fun," she replied and while mid-sentence was already nose back in her book.

He frowned and shook his head, while whispering to himself, 'quite.'

She heard him repeat that word, and as she watched him walk away thought about it for a moment. What a strange twist of fate brought them together in the first place.

He was home schooled, and so was she, that was true, but he didn't tell her right away that his home was the North Pole. In fact, he didn't tell her until the day before they got married.

They met at Camp Minnetonka when they were both eight years old. He was shy, she was outgoing, He had bright white hair it was intriguing, her hair was jet black, so dark it was scary to him, if ever opposites were to attract this was it. They sat next to each other on the bus from the train station to the lake on the very first day, they were both nervous about being around a bunch of other kids that they didn't know, and mostly what they didn't know was how to even be *around* a bunch of other kids, it was frightening. All the rambunctiousness and noise.

All it took was one word to break the ice. She liked marbles and had a whole collection at home, showed him her favorite, a cat's eye the size of a jawbreaker, the iris in the middle was sky blue, almost the color of his eyes, it was weird she said as she put the marble up by his eyeball to compare. He pulled out a marble from his pocket, also the size of a jawbreaker but clear glass, but then he shook it and gave it to her to study and as she looked deep into the glass there were snowflakes swirling about even though it was solid glass.

"You can have it," he said. "It's a present."

It was the first of many throughout the years.

For some reason he loved to give presents, not all the time, but only at the right time.

Usually once a year, whenever they met on the bus for the annual trip to the camp. He always made her a toy, some type of gift that no one had seen before, unique. A top that sang a song, a kite that lit up in colors, a small toy car that could fit in the palm of your hand with a tiny engine that ran, and a little girl driving it that looked just like her.

She was from the desert in the middle of Nevada, he was from the northern part of Alaska, or so he said.

They went to the summer camp every year without fail, and when it was done went to their separate far-flung homes.

They kept in contact throughout the year by letters, then e-mail, then something called zoom. As they got older, in the last two years of high school, still home schooled, they worked for the camp as assistants, and got a paycheck at the end. And then one day when it was clearly the end of camp, the very last camp they would ever attend, and yet he had still not given her a present.

He never waited till the end of summer camp to give her a present and she wondered if after ten years those days were over. She gave *him* a present on the very first day of that last camp, a small oil-painting he could fit in his backpack that she painstakingly brushed, the model for the painting was a canyon near her home at sunset filled with warm colors, she thought it would help keep his heart warm in the cruel northern winds.

And yet still no present from him, as their last summer camp winded down to the bitter end.

But on the very last day after lunch, sitting in the shade of a sycamore tree by the lake watching the kids in their class locked in a free for all beach party bash, he handed her a little box covered in fine green felt. It was a ring box, of that she was sure, and her heart actually skipped a beat as she held it and then with cautious care slowly opened.

It was a silver band, a slim ring with a jewel set on top, a large sparkling diamond cut perfectly round, that threw off colors of blue, orange, and white from the center and edges.

In every other year for the last ten in a row he'd given her an unusual type of toy. But this was no toy, it was a type of jewelry of the highest order and significance.

He gave her the technical specs.

"It's pure silver, mined from the top of a mountain on the edge of the Rockies. The diamond from a secret cave deep under its base."

She looked at it in wonder, afraid to even touch it.

The technician continued:

"I forged it in the middle of winter, on a dark stormy night with a blizzard bearing down on us, fifty below zero. Forged in a white-hot furnace, then cooled in the icy snow. The diamond was the tricky part though. The original gem was the size of a jawbreaker, dull, imperfect, and raw, and yet somehow in the center was perfection, I just needed a little luck to find it." He beamed, proud of his practical dissertation.

"It's an engagement ring," she said simply. "Isn't there something else that goes along with it? Like a specific question?"

"Oh that," he stammered, shy in front of her, as though he was eight years old once again. He was hesitant.

"Well? Are you asking me to marry you or not?" She was beginning to get angry.

He gulped loudly, his face turning red.

"We can if you want, I'd like that very much. There's just this one tiny little thing you need to know first about me and my family. Something important that you need to see for yourself."

"What is it?" Her anger turned to fear, and yet he was smiling, all his attention on the ring, his great new creation.

"Try it on first," he said excitedly. "Let's see if it fits." A young toy maker again, anxious to see if it worked.

She slid the forged silver and diamond ring onto the ring finger of her left hand, it fit perfect. Then as he was admiring it's look on her slender tan hand, she reached over and kissed him square on the lips and did not let go for quite a time.

"I don't care what it is that you need to show me," she said, tears beading in the corners of her eyes. "You're all I need to know."

Right.

They took a commercial flight to Juneau, and from there wheeled a tiny private plane out of a hanger, and Chris got in behind the wheel."

"You're a pilot?"

He shrugged his shoulders.

"Runs in the family. Sort of a tradition."

They flew. Straight north the compass said, on the dot. Hour after hour, over mountains, flat tundra, long winding rivers and streams.

Chris saw a giant herd of deer and swooped down.

"Check this out," he shouted out with glee as he buzzed by the edges of the herd. "There must be a thousand or more!"

She still wore the ring, not willing to take it off until she saw the great mystery that he was so hesitant to unveil.

"What is it?" she pressed him after two

hours in flight. "Do you live in an igloo? Is your mother a wolf?" Referencing the twins Romulus and Remus in Roman mythology.

He laughed. "No, she's a former miss Poppy Queen. We only marry the best." Then quickly corrected himself. "Or hope to."

After four hours of flying over giant snow-covered mountains, still clinging to their packed ice in the middle of summer the little plane maneuvered around a ridge, then down into a box shaped canyon covered in mist.

"It's always misty here, in the summer during the day, something about the sunlight and snow on the edges of the canyon."

He maneuvered the small bush plane down onto a tiny landing pad the size of a house.

"Well, we're here. It's not really the North Pole, but it's close enough." He led her out of the plane towards the big house, seemingly hewn out of stone, cavernous, topped with green tile, great oak hewn double doors and standing there waiting at the entrance was an older version of Chris, smiling, hands on hips, short white hair and half a white beard, and his mother, plaid dress, white apron, and deep dark hair.

Introductions were made.

Melissa was puzzled. Even though they were out in the middle of nowhere, this all seemed quite normal she thought.

Quite.

Then the elves, unable to contain themselves any longer, came pouring out of the house, a giant swirling tribe of tiny mischievous folk, laughing in high pitched sounds, swirling around her, she nearly fainted. Then as one voice, settled down and sang her a welcome song in an ancient elvish language.

Melissa looked at Chris, eyes wide, mouth agape.

He shrugged his shoulders. "My dad's Santa Claus."

They were married in a small church near Melissa's house. Santa and Mrs. Claus were in attendance, incognito of course.

And there it was, in that little town in the desert that they lived for a time.

Chris worked at a bakery in town, while Melissa went to the local college for a nursing degree.

A few quiet years went by, then one day Chris got a call. His dad slipped on some ice and had a fall, and he needed to come home to help with the family business. And that was that.

6.

Down at the edge of the beach it was packed, Chris did a quick calculation as though he were looking out at a sea of presents spread out across the factory, wrapped and ready to be packed into the bags. He counted one hundred at a time and estimated there to be fifty-five groups of that amount. Five thousand five hundred plus, he whistled and then counted the surfers and swimmers in the blue water. Three hundred at least he decided, although it was harder to determine the exact amount since they were always moving about, diving under foamy breakers, riding waves and paddling over others.

At the edge of the hotel where the sand met concrete, sat two long tables next to a row of long surfboards in racks.

Chris studied the operation. First of all, even though they were supposedly beach boys, some of them were older men like himself with big pot bellies, although much tanner, some also slender, still very tan, with grey hair, and some of them girls and women working right alongside. It didn't' seem right to refer them all as beach boys but he wasn't here to judge or pre-judge or convey opinions. He was just here to find Bull.

Their method seemed simple, and like the head of a factory that he was, their process seemed to work like a conveyor belt, the concept was the same whether in the toy factory of at the beach here in Waikiki.

A single tourist or a fresh group of them would approach the table and fill out a form, pay with cash or a card and after receiving instructions, grab a surfboard and head out to the ocean.

Meanwhile others, with wet mottled hair dragging the boards behind them, energy spent and tired, returned them to the rack.

All the workers seemed friendly to each other, smiling, and laughing. Telling each other jokes. It seemed like a happy place to work.

Chris picked up his slippers and trudged onto the beach barefooted, grains of sands crunching between his toes. Too slowly he sensed that the sand was like a skillet sizzling in the heat of the sun, and soon the bottom of his feet seemed to be some sort of food sizzling in that pan. He held back a yelp and tossed the slippers down and slid his toes back in place just in the nick of time.

Some locals nearby, wise to his predicament nodded in appreciation of his technique and he shrugged his shoulders and trudged forward to the table.

The workers saw him approaching, and with a little apprehension asked him if he wanted to rent a board. Chris was very large, and looked like he'd never been on a surfboard, or anywhere near the beach for matter in his entire life.

"Would you like to rent an umbrella, or a surfboard sir?" asked the youngest one, hoping beyond all hope that this big white tourist wasn't going to try to rent a board and then they'd have to rescue him.

"Maybe another time, thank you," he replied courteously with a big sunny smile. "I'm looking for a Mr. Bull Kaupea. Do any of you know him?"

Chris's astute sense noted relief when he said he wasn't going to rent a board, and then a tiny bit of apprehension in their attitude when he asked about Bull.

Maybe it was just that they were business competitors, or maybe it was something more personal. At any rate, they all together as one hesitated, then the oldest and biggest of them with the big belly that rivaled Chris's pointed down the beach, to another table with umbrellas and surfboards.

"He works down there."

Chris's heart sank a notch. 'Down there' looked to be about ten miles away, even though it was probably only a couple of hundred yards.

The big worker noted the look on Chris's face and had pity on him.

"It'll be easier to walk on the sidewalk down there or go down by the hard sand next to the water. Bruddah, you'll never make it walking in slippers in this soft sand."

By the time he got to the next table, Chris was just about ready to call it quits.

Just the day earlier he'd flown around the world in an open sleigh, gotten a few hours rest then flew coach from midnight till this morning. Walked to Kapahulu, then halfway back. Now like Moses in the middle of the desert sands he was huffing and puffing trying to make it the last few feet to the promised land, the beach boy tent.

Maybe it was a rule, but here in this tent was another older beach boy, tan, and good looking, bare chested, grey haired and just about as big as Chris wearing sunglasses, a big coconut leaf hat, and overseeing the operation by sitting back in a big chair leaning against the tent pole.

He nodded with a respect that Chris realized seemed to be prevalent here in the islands. If you were a big boy, and Chris was definitely big, you got some sort of instant recognition from the other big boys. It was kind of like being in a club. And since Chris was used to being around elves that were a fifth his size it was something of a relief. He nodded back to the beach boy.

"Hey howzit brah," said Chris. "What's da scoop?"

"Cherry," said the kanaka.

Chris reached out and gave him the bruddah bruddah handshake.

The kanaka was impressed, but with his sunburned white skin it was obvious that this guy was not from around here.

"Eh brah, where you from?"

Chris decided not to mess around, he needed answers. "Alaska," he said.

"So, what you like, surfboard? Canoe ride?"

"I'm looking for Bull Kaupea."

The kanaka looked at him with a quizzical eye.

"Bully? How come?"

"Friend of mine told me to look him up and tell him howzit, I went by his house but I guess he's on vacation?"

The kanaka nodded.

"Every year, same time, like clockwork. Put it on the calendar brah, the day after Christmas he's outta here." He clapped his hands together with the top one shooting forward.

"You know where I can find him?"

"Nah, I don't know, he's got a big family, scattered all around the islands. He bops all over the place."

"Dang," said Chris. "I really need to find him."

The kanaka could see the genuine concern on Chris's face and had pity on him. He snapped his fingers.

"Hey, you know who might know where he's at is Romeo. He's Bull's cousin. He's out in the water giving surf lessons." He pointed out into the ocean. "Middle of the pack, you see the guy with the coconut hat and sunglasses pushing those tourists in blue rash guards into the waves?"

Chris squinted and nodded.

"Great, I'll wait for him."

"Suit yourself. But he just got out there. The

classes are an hour long."

Chris sighed. It looked too far to swim.

"No problem, I'll paddle out there."

"When's the last time you were on a surfboard?"

"Never. But I can ski and snow board. Looks easy."

"Right," said the kanaka, his voice trailing off. He looked at the rack of boards and shouted out to one of the beach boys: "Eh Kimo! Grab da ten-footer for uncle!" Then he looked over at Chris again and frowned. "Make dat da twelve footah!" He nodded at Chris. "Ten dollars for the hour. You gotta sign the waiver. No worries, we'll be watching out for you."

Now it was Chris's turn to frown. After all he just got done flying a sleigh around the entire planet in one night. How hard could *this* be?

For one thing getting the dang board to the water was a pain. He tried putting it under his arm like everyone else seemed to do it, but this giant board they gave him was so wide and awkward that he couldn't fit it under his armpit and stretch his fingers over the rail.

He tried putting it on top of his head, but again the board was so large that any tiny puff of air from the trade wind threatened to topple him board and all into the crowds that filled the beach. Finally, he decided to just grab the fin on the back of the board and drag it to the water.

After being in the mountains trudging through ice and snow most of the year, seeing water that wasn't frozen, yet alone touching it was a pure treat.

First toes in the wet sand, then feet splashing forward into the soft water, up to knees then waist high dragging the board easily now unfettered by land, floating, lapping on the surface, the water was a perfect temperature, with one hand holding the rail of the board he plunged full body under the water, opening his eyes, misty bubbles from the waves swirling around him, the board nearly got away from him, a row of white water about half a foot high nearly snatched it from his grasp, then he remember the leash and wrapped the Velcro tight around his ankle.

Now the tough part. He watched everyone on their boards out on the ocean and around him by the shore. Some of them made it look easy, while others looked like for lack of a better word, 'kooks'.

Chris did not want to be a kook. Like sledding in the mountains back home, or tubing behind the boat on the lake during summer camp, he summoned up muscle memory, took a deep breath and slid his whole body on the board, head to toes and promptly slid right off the other side.

Some local kids were watching him and they laughed good naturedly. He winced, blubbering, wiping water from his face with a grin.

"You gotta go like this," said a young boy around five, and showed how easy it was to jump belly first onto his boogie board and paddle with both hands one in front of the other in rhythm.

Chris tried again, slower this time, slid his big belly onto the board, holding onto the rails to steady himself at the front end, toes straddling the tail, success! He yelped with laughter and began to paddle out into the ocean and then the first foamy wave hit him square tumbling him over on his back, still holding onto the board for dear life, he struggled back to the surface, holding onto the board with his arm stretched over the deck, in dismay.

"It's no use. I'm a kook," he whispered.

Deciding that it was easier to just walk out there dragging the board next to him through the water he did just that.

The water was still shallow and for the most part all sand and turned out to be the easier of the two options. He came up with a brilliant plan.

Whenever a rolling wave of foam came his way, and it was every few seconds now, he'd continue holding onto the board, then duck his whole weight under, and he was in effect like a sea anchor, unbudgeable, it was a great idea, until he got closer to the surf school and was just about to say a greeting to Romeo, when a larger set of waves appeared, the ocean here was a bit deeper, he had a tougher time getting his balance before the roller hit the board and the first wave tried to bend him sideways, he lost his straight line, and the worst thing it turned out was to be caught sideways on a buoyant surfboard, in front of a wall of foam.

The double thick twelve-foot board was the size of two normal boards and packed that much more punch.

The next wave hit him, seemingly with the power of a small avalanche, and three-hundred-pound sea anchor or not the board was caught at the front of the churning foam and kept in place by the incredible buoyancy.

Ten normal men couldn't hold it back placed square as it was in front of the rolling white water of doom.

Chris held on with great might but was dragged behind what was in effect a twelve-foot-wide hard as a rock, epoxy broom, a bulldozer surfboard mowing down the surf school and everyone else in its path. Still Chris held on and was tumbled once more over the board, holding on mightily until board and body finally separated, board going one way, and body to the other. The one lucky break was the leash held tight and true, and saved more poor surfers in the boards path from its cruel punishment.

Chris looked back at his path of destruction; eight surfers turned swimmers from getting decimated by Chris. He waved his hand while grimacing, "Sorry!"

"Hey!" Romeo yelled. "Hold onto your board!"

The sea calmed down, and Chris was able to make his way closer to Romeo. He shook his head.

"Dang haoles," said Chris, joking around.

"Whatchu doing brah, come over on this side," said the instructor, then chuckled loudly good-naturedly. "Dang haoles is right."

Chris did as he was told and circled around to the other side while the instructor barked out instructions to his small group of learners, coaxing them to paddle hard through the little channel back where he stood on the reef. They hovered in little groups just outside his reach, and then one by one he would grab onto the nose of their board, line them up, give last minute directions, and when a swell came upon steadily and gently launch them in front of the sloping wave, giving them a head start and speed on the swell.

"Up! Up!" he'd shout watching them to make sure they did as told, then he'd reach back for the next victim.

There was a lull in the action as all his students were way inside the foamy water, so he looked over at Chris.

"What's up brah, howzit."

A friendly native.

Chris tried to sit on the board like all the other people around him seemed to be doing, it looked pretty easy, but he was like a cork, lost his balance, tipped over upside down, came up blubbering, and gave up, standing on the reef holding onto the rail of the board.

"Guy on the beach, Kanaka, told me to come ask you about Bull Kaupea."

"Yeah, what about him? That's my cousin."

"I'm a friend of a friend, just wanted to say hi, I mean howzit, but I heard he's on vacation."

"Oh yeah, he wen holoholo."

Chris narrowed his eyes. Hawaiian.

"What's that?"

"Holoholo brah, he went to go look around. Hawaiian style."

"Do you know where?"

"All over this island, and maybe some outer islands too. Not really sure. He didn't give me his exact itinerary if that's what you mean. You see he works hard all year, day after day, giving surf lessons to take care of his family, on a tight schedule, gotta pay da bills, right? But once a year he puts everything on the side, all work, all timeclocks, takes his family and goes holoholo, go spock it out, no commitments. Basically, he goes around to see our family, reconnect with the ohana. They're all over the place."

"Dang," said Chris. "So, you don't know where he went? Maybe I can look in the phone book for Kaupea and call around."

"Good luck with that brah. He did tell me one thing though. His first stop is up in Waianae."

Chris repeated the name slowly. "Why-ah-nigh."

"Yeah, Waianae brah. Actually, just before you get there. Look for a sign that says Lualualei and take a right. I don't know exactly where it is though. Tough place, you better be careful you go there." Romeo narrowed his eyes. What in the world was he getting this haole into? "In fact, now that I think about it better you don't even go."

"Tougher than out here?" Chris looked around at tourists wiping out right and left.

"Yeah brah, it's tougher than out here. Anyways, he said he was going to the chicken fights first to see our cousins Benny and Kimo. After that, I don't know, he likes to travel with the wind. Bumbye, you wait till he gets back; it'll just be a couple of days."

"I won't be here that long. Gotta get back to work. But thanks for the tip," said Chris and got ready to walk the board back in.

"Whoa brah wait a minute. No do the paddle of shame."

"What's that?"

"When you don't catch a wave and just paddle in. Empty handed."

"I was gonna walk."

"Same thing, only worse, I think. Come over here big bruddah. Any friend of Bulls is a friend of mine, lay down on the board, I'll hold it steady. Now listen, when I say 'UP', you jump up to your feet, don't drag your knees, put your hands down hard on the top of the board, jump up quick and get in the sumo wrestler stance, okay? One foot in front of the other. You snow board yeah?"

"I tear it up."

"What foot forward works best?"

Chris thought for a moment, envisioning it in his mind.

"Right foot forward."

"You're a goofy foot." Romeo shrugged his shoulders. "Anyways, that's what we call it in surfing. Regular foot is left foot forward."

"I'm a goofy foot," smiled Chris. "My wife would agree with that."

The surf students were straggling in and around Romeo. It was time to go.

"Here comes a set," he said. "You ready?"

Chris nodded. "I got this."

"Okay, here we go," said Romeo and tried to push Chris into the wave, then realized he needed some extra umph to get the big man going, grimaced and pushed mightily, the giant board glided in front of the swell. "UP! UP!" he shouted, and from the back of the wave he first saw Chris' head, then shoulders and arms in the sumo crouch.

"He's got it," said Romeo. "Dang big haole's got it."

Chris stood tall on the board, the heck with the sumo crouch, smiling from ear to ear, speed under his feet, board chattering on the water. He turned back to look at Romeo, and pointed at him, then gave the shaka.

"Watch where you're going big bruddah," he whispered, then shouted: "WATCH WHERE YOU'RE GOING!"

Too late, and it wouldn't have mattered anyways if he watched where he was going.

Chris enjoyed the feeling of going fast on the board, but realized that he couldn't turn it, or stop it, not one single notch, and dead ahead, literally, and figuratively was a pack of floundering surf schoolers right in his path.

Romeo saw arms waving like propellers on a plane, and he winced in knowledge of what was coming next, a giant splash of water in front of the wave, the big board flipping up in the air, along with others nearby as a platoon of surfers ditched their boards to try to avoid disaster. It was a wipeout of epic proportions on a two-foot wave in Waikiki.

Then Romeo smiled when the white water cleared away and he could see that everyone was safe, all heads above water. Chris waved back at him and started paddling in, one wave and done.

Then Romeo winced as he thought about big bruddah going up to Waianae. And then he chuckled and smiled. No way was he gonna find the chicken fights anyways so there was no need to worry.

7.

Chris decided to rent a car at the front desk and chose a little red sedan.

Getting out of Waikiki was slow going, but once he got on the freeway, it was smooth sailing and he was headed for the west side. Nanakuli, passed some type of power plant, then Maili point, down a long straight stretch of highway next to the ocean, and stopped in front of a row of stores on the outskirts of the little town, near a sign that said Lualualei.

Now what, thought Chris. There wasn't going to be a sign pointing to the chicken fight arena. You wouldn't find it on a map.

A middle-aged woman was walking from the store carrying a bag of groceries.

"Excuse me ma'am, do you know where the chicken fights are located?"

She squinted her eyes suspiciously at him and kept walking without a word. It was useless.

He spotted a young boy around five years old watching him carefully from the safety of his brand-new bike with training wheels. He patted on the handlebars and pointed at Chris.

Even though the magic of Christmas morning was many hours and days past, the glow still enveloped Chris / Santa for those that believed. This young boy must have gotten a present from someone proclaiming to be Santa as often times happened, and the aura of the man prevailed over the lack of white beard and red suit.

"Nice bike," he said while kneeling down at a distance, giving the young man plenty of room. The boy just nodded, stunned.

"Can you talk?"

That's all it took. The icebreaker.

"I'm in kindergarten. Miss Jones class."

"That's fantastic. You must have bikes and blocks and books to read. Do you take naps?"

The boy laughed. "Those are for babies."

Chris smiled. "So, you work all day long. That's great. How many friends do you have?"

He looked down at his hand and started counting starting with his thumb and then over into the fingers.

"Well, there's Mac, and Koa, and Mika, and Blaze, and..." he thought for a moment and decided on one more. "... and Clarissa."

"So, Mac must be your best friend since you said his name first." He wanted to ask if Clarissa was his girlfriend but that would have been taking their new friendship down the wrong road.

"One last question and I'll let you get back to riding that new bike. Do you know if there's a chicken fight arena in this town? And if so where it's located?"

The little boy thought hard and pointed towards a short hill in the distance.

Chris followed a dirt road lined with scrub brush, and came to an old factory, broken down and discarded, with a square warehouse on the side. Cars and trucks were parked everywhere on the outside on the hard scrabble road, and it was not apparent where exactly the entrance of this event was located.

Somewhere in the middle of this old, dilapidated warehouse was the distant roar of a small crowd yelling and cheering at a sporting event.

As Chris poked his head through the tin doorway, he heard a sound behind him and turned to see a short yet round and tough looking man with a grizzled face and mean squint in his eyes.

"Eh Brah, whatchu doing ovah hea?"

"What? Bodda you?" said Chris without missing a beat.

Now even though Chris was getting the hang of pidgin slang, the situations in which you used certain terminology, certain phrases varied by circumstance. His friend at the bus stop forgot to tell him some small details.

There were some things you didn't say to strangers in Hawaii if you wanted to avoid a beating.

For instance, if someone tells you 'What', you don't say 'What?' back. And you don't add insult by way of asking if it 'Boddas' or bothers them, because then you're just asking for trouble. It's like putting a piece of wood on your shoulder and daring them to knock it off.

Chris was just joking of course and testing out his pidgin but it didn't go over very well.

The short mean man threw down the towel in his hand and picked up a shovel that was leaning against the wall and walked slowly forward.

"Yeah, as a matter-of-fact fat man, it does bodda me. So, you like beef."

Key words.

"No, no, no" Chris repeated, but the short mean man kept moving forward with the shovel.

Chris made a quick note. This guy was definitely on the naughty list, and probably had been since birth. The shovel whistled by Chris's head as he ducked quickly and hustled to the side. Blocked by the wall, he considered two options, cry for mercy which probably wouldn't work or fight back. As the shovel whistled by his head again and clanked against the wall throwing sparks, he decided for the second option and rushed forward closing the distance so the mean guy didn't have enough room to swing the shovel, grabbed his wrist with one hand, looped his other arm under the elbow and locked that hand onto his own forearm in an arm bar and cranked down until the mean guys face was in the dirt, yelling in pain and fear.

"Don't break it, please don't break it, I give up!"

"You gonna be good?" asked Chris.

"Yes! Yes!"

"You gonna be nice?"

"Yes, yes I'll be nice!"

"Cause I aint gonna ask you twice."

The mean guy had a quizzical look on his face as he turned in pain to stare at his tormentor with bug eyes.

"I promise!"

"Okay den," said Chris and unhooked his vice grips then stood up a safe distance away.

The mean guy sat where he was and rubbed his forearm.

"Damn crazy haole. This is private property, whatchu doin' snooping around?"

"I'm looking for the chicken fights."

The mean guy's eyes narrowed suspiciously.

"Aint no chicken fights around here man. Those are illegal. What are you a cop?"

Chris chuckled. "No, I'm not a cop." Even though I know who's naughty and who's nice, he thought. "I'm actually not even looking for the chicken fights, I'm just looking for someone who might be *at* the chicken fights."

"Oh yeah? Who dat."

"Bull Kaupea."

His eyes narrowed even further. "How you know him?"

"We're old friends. He's Kainani's dad. I'm just here visiting from Alaska. I heard he came this way."

"Shoots brah! Why didn't you say dat in da first place? That's my cousin."

The mean guy's face turned into a happy face, beaming smile from ear to ear. He blushed in embarrassment as he got quickly to his feet and held out his hand.

Chris gave him the bruddah bruddah handshake that he learned in Waikiki.

"What's your name anyways?"

"Chris."

"I'm Benny, glad to meet you. Sorry about the shovel."

"Yeah, sorry about the arm-bar."

"They teach you that shit up in Alaska?"

"Ju jitsu? Yeah, never know when you're going to run into an angry lumber jack, or polar bear for that matter." He forgot he was under cover for a moment. "One of the elves runs a class once a week…" He stopped as Benny eyed him.

"One of the elves?"

"Sorry I mumbled. Not elves. I meant yelves. It's a nick name we give the Ju jitsu instructors we have up there. They're kind of small like a elf, but when they put you in an arm bar you yell. Get it?"

"Yeah, I get it," mumbled Benny as he rubbed his arm. "Yelves. Classic. You guys from Alaska are a riot. Anyways, Bull's not here. He came through to say hello to everyone like he does every year with his wife and daughter, and he left."

"Dang. Know where he went?"

"North shore I think is his next stop. You might check auntie Tia, his sistah. She lives up by Pupukea. He's making the rounds on Oahu, then they go to the outer islands. I think anyways, he didn't really say. Hey, you want to come inside and see the chicken fights while you're here?"

"I thought you said there weren't any?"

"C'mon man," he laughed, "we gotta be careful. It's a cultural thing, but not everyone approves."

Chris shook his head no. His naughty list was already pretty full and he didn't want to add to it while on vacation. He reached out and gave Benny the bruddah bruddah.

"Pupukea?"

"Just past the old gas station. You like to eat good food."

Chris frowned with his palms up near his belly that was rounding out his t-shirt.

Benny laughed. "Yeah, me too." Patting his own substantial tummy. "When you get up there just follow your nose, you'll find the house. Auntie Tia, she makes the most ono grinds on the island. Broke da mouth."

Chris squinted, tilting his head in the universal body language of 'what?'

Bennie laughed. "Her food is so good that when you take a bite, your mouth goes all jello all stoked."

"Broke da mouth," Chris repeated as he walked away. It was almost lunchtime and his stomach was beginning to rumble.

"Go past Waimea, past Sharks Cove, you'll see the ocean on the left, go past an old gas station on the right then a couple of houses down you'll see a little blue house."

"You don't know the address, do you?"

"No need. Brah you can't miss it."

8.

On the north side of the island in the little bit of a town just outside Pupukea sat an old sugar plantation house with a big porch in the front and surfboards lined along the side, and in the front yard

The phone rang in the kitchen and the woman cooking at the stove reached over and picked it up.

"Hello?"

"Hey auntie Tia, this is cousin Kimo."

"Hey what's up cuz?" she shouted at the phone. Calling someone cuz was a nice gesture in Hawaii, and in this case it was true, Kimo really was her cousin, way over on the west side of the island in Waianae.

"Not much, we're cruzin' over here. Had a good Christmas?"

"Oh yeah."

"Hey is Bull there?"

"Yeah, they just got here a little while ago, he's out talking story with Koa, Mel's at work.

"Can I talk to him?"

"Shoots cuz." She put the phone down and went back to the stove to continue stirring the pot and yelled towards the front door: "Bully!, Bully boy, phone call! It's cousin Kimo!" Then muttered to herself. "Probably just wants a surf report."

A large man opened the front door and walked into the kitchen. At six foot four and two hundred plus with a Hawaiian war club tattooed on his right bicep, not many people would even think about messing with him. But to his sister Tia he was just a big teddy bear, her baby brother that she could still tickle into submission. He came into the kitchen acting like a big hound dog following his nose, sniffing the air looking for food, then slyly slid his hand over a big spoon laying on the side and made as though he was going to dip it into the pot for a little tasty taste.

Tia slapped him on the wrist. POW. And he dropped the spoon, grimacing with real pain on his face.

"Hey, that really hurt!"

"You know da rules. No tasty taste till pau."

Which meant quite simply, no snacking on auntie Tia's creation until it was finished to perfection. He scrunched up his face but she just narrowed her eyes at him. It was a draw.

Bull went over to the phone and picked it up.

"Hey cuz what's up?"

"What, you guy's going surf?"

"I don't know cuz, it's pretty small. You coming over?"

"Naw, I gotta work. The reason I called is there's this big haole guy looking for you."

"Whatchu mean one big haole guy?"

"Yeah, brah, he came to the chicken fights this morning a little after you left. Benny thought he was a cop and tried to rough him up, but *he* was da guy got roughed up."

Bull scoffed out loud.

"Why in the heck would Benny try to rough someone up if he thought he was a cop? What's wrong with that guy?"

"Ahh, it's Benny. You know how he is, kinda loco. Trying to protect the operation, I guess. Anyways, this big haole guy told him he was a friend and needed to talk with you. So, Benny told him you were heading up to Tia's house, 'cause it was sort of a tradition."

"It is. And why would I care if some big haole guy is trying to find me. I have plenty of haole friends, some of them are big, and I got nothing to hide anyways."

"The way Benny described him; I don't think this guy is one of your normal haole friends."

"What do you mean 'normal haole'?"

"Well, this guy is about three hundred plus."

"Ho that's a big boy,"

"...and he has short stubby white hair like he's old, but he moves fast as a cat, his skin is whiter than typing paper, but he's got a fresh sunburn on his cheeks and forearms."

Bull nodded knowingly. "Fresh off the boat."

"That's right Bull, he's a big haole man fresh off the boat and he's looking for you."

"Maybe it's some tourist dude I gave a surf lesson to, and he's back in the islands. I can't remember anyone that big, not three hundred pounds. Back when the Pro Bowl was played at

Aloha Stadium, we'd get some big guys come down to try surfing, but I always take my vacation when they're here."

"Anyways, that's why I called. AND to check on the surf."

"It's pretty flat. We're having lunch here and then heading east."

"Dang, k-den talk to you later." said Kimo and Bull reached over the counter and hung up the phone.

He tilted his head squinting his eyes, deep in thought and murmured, "hmmm"

Tia, being an inquisitive person and a wahine to boot was intrigued.

"Some big haole guy looking for you?"

"Three hundred plus with a bald head and white skin and hair." He smiled. "Maybe he's from the world wrestling federation and needs some new talent." He snapped his fingers, his face getting serious. "Or *maybe* he's from a talent agency and wants to put me in a movie!"

"Maybe he heard about you talking stink about someone in his family and came over to bust you up."

"Crazy? No one's gonna bust *me* up." He flexed his Hawaiian bicep with the war club tattoo. "Plus, you know me sis, I don't talk stink about no one. I am pure aloha."

"Yeah right..." muttered Tia.

"Hey," said Bull as he pointed to the back of the house while subtly sliding his hand back to a big idle spoon. "What's that mangy cat doing in the house?"

Tia took the bait and looked quickly down

the hall. That dang cat was always finding a way to sneak into the house.

In the corner of her eye, she saw Bull try to scoop a bit of stew from the pot but she was still too fast for him and popped him on the back of his head with her big wooden spoon and kept on popping as he yelped towards the front door and safety.

Out on the porch Leilani and Kainani were sitting on a swinging bench in the shade. The porch itself looked out over a wide green lawn that stretched out to a busy roadway, and beyond that was the ocean. The white sand from the beach encroaching up onto the black tar. Cars with surfboards on top lined the road here and there, with young surfers, tan and lean, leaning against tires, hoods and bumpers. No one was moving very fast. The waves were flat.

"The waves are flat," said Koa, a fifteen something surfer with long black hair-tinged gold on the ends. Kainani's cousin. He leaned against porch railing looking out towards the sea, shaking his head. Dejected.

Kainani reached out with a long stick and brushed it against his bare ankle, yelling "Centipede!"

Koa jumped in the air with a sharp yelp, whirling around, swatting at his legs, and saw Kainani laughing.

"You buggah!" he shouted, leaped over her, and pretended to pound her into submission.

"Koa!" shouted Tia as she came out onto the porch.

"Yeah, but mom..."

"It's okay, I can take it," laughed Kainani. She secretly wished she had a little brother to tease and have him tease back.

"So," asked auntie Tia to Kainani sitting down next to her. "Did you get everything you wanted for Christmas?"

Kainani scrunched her face. "Well..." the word stretched out into a question mark. She grabbed her mom's arm next to her face, wrapping her own arms around it and kissed, kissed, kissed it.

"This is my present."

Tia narrowed her eyes; she knew something was up.

"C'mon, spill it out."

Kainani knew she was trapped.

"Well, I wanted a doll, and I got that, and I wanted a new dress and new shorts and got both of those..." Her voice trailed off. Her face wasn't sad, it had a slight tinge, a vague look of disappointment that somehow is acquired by people, children when they get to be this age.

"Eh," said Bull. "That's everything that was on the list."

"That's a pretty short list," said Tia.

"It wasn't on the list," Kainani said simply. "That's okay."

She knew that her parents worked hard to support them. The rent was high, food was expensive. She could hear them talking when they thought she was asleep. She really didn't want anything for herself, just for them to be happy.

"Not on the list?" pressed her dad. "How's anyone supposed to know?"

She pulled auntie Tia closer and whispered in her ear. "I wished for a present from Santa."

"Oh," Tia said.

"What?" asked her dad.

"It's okay," said Kainani. "You can tell him."

"She wished for a secret present from Santa," said Tia, raising her eyebrows.

"Oh," said her dad. He was also holding onto youth and innocence as long as he could, not wanting his daughter to grow up too fast, and not willing to be the one to throw cold water on the magic of Christmas.

"Oh well," he continued. "That's the way it goes sometimes, I guess. Better luck next year." Trying to cheer her up. "Maybe he couldn't find our house, or the reindeer got tired and they had to cut their trip short."

"Maybe he found out you were being mean to your cousin," said Koa. "And he put you on the naughty list."

Kainani stuck her tongue out at him.

"See, exactly what I mean."

"What about you Leilani," asked Tia. "Did you get everything you wanted for Christmas."

Kainani's mom Leilani seemed to be daydreaming. In her early thirties, hapa haole Irish, Filipino, Chinese, she was radiant with her brown hair tied in a bun at the back of her head, eyes drifting, watching the birds in the trees.

Kainani patted her mom's arm lightly. She knew that she was still tired from a long week of working at the hotel.

"Did you get everything that you wanted for Christmas mommy?"

Leilani snapped out of her dream, and smiled sweetly with a sigh, turned and hugged Kainani while looking over at Bull.

"I got everything I need right here."

Koa frowned. This was a little too syrupy for him.

"What did uncle Kimo have to say Mom, are the waves up on the west side?"

"He didn't say, called to tell Bull that some big haole guy was looking for him."

"Oh yeah?" He turned to face the big man. "Uncle Bull?"

"I don't know," said Bull. "Probably some tourist that needs a surf lesson from da best."

"Three hundred plus, with white skin, and white hair," said Tia.

Kainani thought hard, it couldn't be, could it?

"Maybe he's da repo man," said Koa. "Coming for get you brah!"

"He's not the repo man," said Bull. "Now stop it."

"You want me to pound him, just say the word uncle Bull," said Koa, while punching his fist into his palm.

"What do you weigh now?" asked Bull. "One fifty, one fifty-five?"

"One fifty-seven," said Koa, nodding his head with self-confidence.

"We'll need two of you then. Plus, no one's pounding anyone, it's still Christmas."

"I'm here for you whenever you need me," said Koa, acting the tough guy.

"Well great," said Bull with a smile. "Because Kimo told him that we're here at Tia's house. He'll probably be here soon."

That sobered up young Koa quick, and he looked towards the road. "Well, you're going to be here, right uncle Bull?"

"Wrong. As soon as we eat auntie Tia's soup, we gotta hit the highway."

He tried to make a break for it, but Tia was quicker, jumping to her feet and blocking the doorway with the wooden spoon like a warclub.

"Five minutes," she said. "Relax."

Bull nodded, backing up with hands in the air in surrender, and continued to Koa whose whole persona had turned stone cold serious.

"When you see the big haole guy, tell him we went to the east side. Our next stop is Kaawa, cousin Sean's pig hunt."

9.

Meanwhile, back at Santa's workshop it was pure and total mayhem. Unfettered by the absence of both Santa and Mrs. Claus at the very same time they were running amok.

If Santa and Mrs. Claus knew what was going on, (and they probably did) they would shrug their shoulders and pay it no mind. They were after all on vacation, and the elves deserved a little break as well.

The pressures and deadlines of meeting their quota for Christmas day had them all wound up with energy that couldn't just come to a complete stop. They would after all like any tight wound ball eventually pop.

Elves were naturally full of bursting energy after all, harnessed and focused with a clear objective at hand they were unmatched by any machine or mechanized robotic manufacturing plant. They could work all day and night with only candy for food, and sometimes a few donuts thrown in as well.

Without a chief, a head of state, a supervisor to advise them and present a calm order, it was chaos.

Two of the young elves were having a contest to see who could swing farther on the wagon wheel chandeliers hanging high up and straight down from the cavernous ceiling.

While down below them a makeshift bowling alley was constructed with yellow slip and slides lined up next to each other, lathered with baby oil, the pins to be knocked over rows of brass bells of all shapes and sizes, and whoever made the biggest sound was the winner. The bowling ball replacements flung down the lanes were young elves with football helmets, the technique was such: Four other elves would each grab an arm and a leg each, and then with a one, and a two, and a three race towards the plastic slides and fling the young elves down the chutes.

The funny part that made them all roll with laughter and glee as they played that game, was that after smashing through the bells and making quite the clatter, there was nothing to stop the poor little elves forward momentum, covered in baby oil they kept sliding right across the wood floor crashing into the wall.

Suddenly, a shadow appeared at the front door. All the elves got quiet. The chandeliers above them stopped swinging, and there was just a tiny squeak from the chains. You could hear a pin drop. It was the big cheese, the top dog, the capo de capo, the big enchilada, the hot tamale, you name it.

When Mr. and Mrs. Claus were gone, he was the boss, and don't think for a minute that he didn't know it.

At four foot eight he towered over the rest of the elves. Every company, every operation needed an enforcer, and this elf was it. Chiseled face, piercing eyes, tall, pointed ears, bald head, swarthy puffed out chest, he was an imposing figure. He strode into the great room slowly, methodically taking in the whole wretched scene with a scowl on his face. If only he had a whip and a bullhorn it would complete the whole package.

"What's going on here?" he asked calmly with a measured voice, eyes searching the room for anyone brave enough with an answer.

The younger elves looked at their feet, while the older elves just looked on with trepidation tinged with regret, fear. Shaking their heads.

No one seemed to know what was 'going on'.

He walked over to the nearest elf standing at the foot of the slippey slide waiting his turn to be thrown to the wall. With one hand on hip and the other outstretched he commanded the elf.

"Gimme that helmet."

The elf complied meekly, slowly removing it and handing it over, eyes down.

"You have no idea what you're doing, do you?"

The other elf shook his head while the big kahuna elf put the helmet onto his own head.

"I'll show you how it's done," he said as he reached out his hands and outstretched his legs to four elves on the side, then said to them. "C'mon guys. A one and a two..."

"AND A THREE!" they all shouted grabbing

onto the head elf, each with a limb, swinging once back for momentum, and flinging him, flopping him on his chest with all their might down the slide.

The head elf yelled like a banshee as he barreled down the yellow tarmac towards the bells, then halfway there jumped to his slippery feet still sliding, gaining forward speed with less drag, crouched, knees bent, arms angled for balance like the silver surfer on the toys that they made.

"YEEEAAAAAHHHHH!!!!" he yelled loudly as he crashed through the bells then kept going towards the wall, jumping in the air at the very last moment, feet planted on the wall, then springing off it nimbly, summersault in the air, full twist with a backflip and landed square on both feet, arms outstretched in victory, the whole place erupted in applause.

And that was the reason he was the head elf.

Pandemonium erupted once again, filling the great hall with laughter and loud cheers as the elves all scrambled to get in line to try their hand at this new fun game.

10.

On the north shore Chris went through Haleiwa, past Waimea, past Sharks Cove, and just before Pupukea parked past the old gas station and walked down the road.

Second or third house, Benny said. Can't miss it.

He followed his nose, catching a slight hint, a faint scent of a soup or a stew, it was hard to tell which, but it was one of the two There was a definitive aroma floating on the trade wind that was blowing from the mountains and over the houses towards the sea. He kept walking and the aroma diminished, so he backtracked, right into the center of the invisible stream of wonderful fragrance.

He walked towards the house in a bit of a trance, sublime torture, his stomach rumbled loudly and he patted it. "Quiet now."

A young man of about fifteen came out of the house onto the porch, eyes full of suspicion.

"Mom!" he yelled turning towards the screen door. "The big haole's here!"

Chris kept his composure, no emotion on his face. He was in fact, as he knew, a big haole.

A middle-aged Hawaiian woman came out onto the porch. Her eyes were soft and inquisitive.

"Can we help you?"

Chris was as polite as a butler in the palace to the queen.

"Yes, thank you for asking miss. I'm looking for Bull. His cousin Benny told me I might find him here at your house."

He actually bowed ever so slightly, the aroma of whatever was cooking on the stove nearly overwhelming him.

She saw the look in his eyes and smiled.

"You hungry?"

"Oh yes," Chris gulped, with one hopeful nod of his head.

"Well come inside," she motioned with her hand, then backhanded her son ever so gently. "Mind your manners."

"I'm Chris," he said and put out his hand in the bruddah bruddah.

"Koa," said the young man.

Then Tia put her hand out for a gentle normal handshake and Chris realized at that moment that the bruddah bruddah was probably only between guys.

"I'm Tia, Bull's sister, please come inside."

After the second bowl was wiped clean, Chris sat back and sighed.

"Another one?" asked Tia hopefully.

"Oh no," said Chris. "That was amazing." He thought for a quick moment and continued. "Broke da mouth."

She smiled and took the bowl to the sink. A

quick judge of character, she saw the kindness in his eyes when he first came up towards the house, and trusted he was good.

"You actually just missed them by a few minutes. They went to the east side, to a little town next to Kaneohe. Our cousin lives there. It's a place on this island that's real country."

Chris nodded. To his cousin's house. "I'm finding out that it's a big island, as far as family goes. Do you mind if I ask you what's the name of that soup?"

"Portagee bean soup."

"It's incredible. Can you tell me the recipe, so I can share it with my wife?" he asked hopefully.

But she shook her head with a sly grin.

"Top secret. "You gotta come back here if you want this model. Everyone has their own recipe for this soup. A little extra pinch of this or that."

His face was genuinely sad, she chuckled and had pity on him.

"It's easy. Ham hock, Portuguese sausage, red kidney beans, potatoes, onions, carrots, cabbage, macaroni, tomato sauce, diced tomatoes..."

He leaned forward taking mental notes, tapping on his open palm with a finger as though writing.

"...a little salt and pepper, and whatever else you like. I use a little paprika and Hawaiian salt. To be honest it's never exactly the same every time, just give a little tasty taste as you go and add spice as needed."

He sighed slightly, belly full and happy.

"Thank you for the hospitality, can I help you with the dishes?"

She frowned. "No, that's why we have Koa."

Who scowled on the side.

Chris handed each of them a small gift. Koa got a small wax comb for his surfboard, and Tia a pair of pure silver earrings that resembled thin dangling icicles.

"Wow uncle."

Tia gushed. "These are nice thank you."

"Well, it's technically still Christmas," said Chris, and it was until he delivered that last present, for him it was still going.

"So I guess I'll head south-east?"

"Get back on Kam highway, go east, and head around the island for Kaawa. Right before you get to Swanzy beach park you'll see a big green house on the right. It backs up to the forest and the mountains behind it."

"You know the address?" He wanted to plug it in to his GPS but had a feeling that the address was 'big green house'.

"I don't know the address but it has a bunch of dog kennels out front, that's kind of the marker. Good luck finding them," she said, giving him a big hug at the door. "They move fast. This time of year, they sure like to go holoholo."

11.

"Dey wen go hun pig," blubbered the young lad outside the house on the outskirts of Kaawa.

His voice was broken, and he seemed either on the verge of crying, or had just got done sobbing before Chris got to the house. He pointed up into the hills rising into the clouds. Jungle shrouded valleys rising into the mist.

Chris wanted to make sure he understood what the boy was saying, his brow furrowed, eyes narrowed.

"You mean they went on a pig hunt?"

"Yeah," said the young boy his lower lip trembling as he said it, probably around three or four years old. Chris realized suddenly why he was so upset.

"They wouldn't let you go, would they?"

"No," said the boy, holding back a sob, looking down at his feet, wiping a tear away from his eyes.

"Yeah, I figured as much. Well, someone has to stay behind and take care of the house," said Chris. "They chose you because you're the bravest of all."

The young boy looked up with bright eyes, hopeful that what he was hearing was true.

"That's right," said Chris, nodding knowingly. "Now straighten your back, and hold your head high, no need to worry, no need to cry."

"I wasn't crying," the boy quickly said, correctly the big haole stranger while wiping his eyes with the back of his hand.

"Right you are," said Chris admitting his mistake. "I meant to say no sighing. So just to make sure, Bull, Leilani, and Kainani all went up into the mountains to go hunt pigs."

The boy nodded with wide eyes. There was something about the big haole man that looked familiar...

Chris pulled a little toy out of his pocket and placed it into the small palm. It was a little toy dog, and when you squeezed it, it barked.

The boy smiled and laughed.

And now as Chris climbed through the thick brush, stepping gingerly over moss covered rocks and ferns, somewhere far up in the distance the sound of real barking dogs wafted through the shadows and green leaves, through the cavernous canopy, barking echoing as though the heavy blanket of jungle was a thick fog hiding the source and yet amplifying it.

The sound getting closer and closer, now on the right then the left, then a different sound mixed in the mix, a loud squeal, then another, then a cacophony of yelping squealing pattering of feet, an army of runners running his way, crashing of branches and trees, human yelling now, shouting out dog's names and instructions. There was some cursing also, frantic words yelled in angst.

The roiling ball of noise barreled through the trees and now Chris could see in the near distance the tops of bushes waving, like a avalanche crashing down the mountain, he braced himself instinctively, shoes wedged against rocks, crouched in a defensive position as the boiling landslide of fur, hooves and teeth blasted into the clearing. A churning pack of pigs and piglets, black and brown bristly haired demons were on him in a flash, crashing against his legs wave upon waves, then a big female around a hundred pounds plus couldn't maneuver quick enough and ran straight over Chris, bouncing against his big belly and knocking him sideways to the ground. In the corner of his eye, he saw them now, yawing and barking, nipping at the heels of the beast of all beasts, with a half dozen skinny vicious dogs on his tail. A giant black boar bigger than Chris, four hundred pounds plus, dogs nipping at his hooves, dogs leaping onto his back and latching onto his ears, the beast whipping his jowls with two curved tusk side to side, shedding the dogs, gouging them, yet still they came on him in waves, slowing him down to a slow frantic gallop, straight... into... Chris...

If he wasn't laying on his side with feet askew from the first wave of attackers, then maybe he could have jumped out of the way. As the hairy, stench billowing bulldozer was about to run him over, Chris looked straight into wild, terrified eyes, tusks yellow and black from rooting up the mud with some splatters of dog blood on the edges, a split second from being gored himself, with lightning fast instinct Chris reached up in the nick of time and grabbed onto both tusks, and held on tight for dear life, years of handling reins on Christmas Eve bucking through storms around the world high in the clouds must have trained him for this moment, the bull of a beast boar slid to the side squealing loudly in Chris's face with a breath like the bottom of a pit of filth, Chris held on.

Now yelling in the background, human voices shouting for him to move to the side, they couldn't shoot with him so close, hold your fire! yelled the voices, hold your fire!, and still Chris held on, till with a mighty heave of its beastly neck, the boar heaved Chris to the side, and with him the last two dogs that were latched onto its ears.

"Move haole!" shouted one of the voices but Chris was wedged into a pile of rocks and too tired from wrestling the behemoth to move an inch and he watched from the safety of the ground as the boar crashed through the bushes and was gone.

Half a dozen dogs lay scattered around him, battered, bloodied and bruised. Their fight spent, whimpering in fear perhaps of the wrath of their masters more than the pain from the hooves and tusks.

Two hunters stood over Chris, dressed in camouflage and cradling rifles.

"You okay?" asked the smaller one, while the

bigger one just shook his head.

"Yeah, sorry to get in the way." He got slowly to his feet, backside bruised with a small cut on his right elbow and knee that took the brunt of the fall on the rocks. As he bent down to pick up the little sack with the present inside, one of the dogs sniffed at it, probably smelling the scent of the reindeer. It barked once then grabbed at the bag and tried to make off with it, snarling and biting down on the package, and turning to run. Chris went down to the ground again, wrestling with the dog, a tug of war ensued, the mutt had a firm grip with teeth firm on the red cloth, growling and shaking it.

"Hey!" shouted Chris as the cloth began to rip in between slobbery jowls, shaking it like a chew toy. Another dog jumped in and now there were two mongrel hounds tearing at the bag with the precious cargo inside. Chris battled the two beasts, sure to lose the war.

It was comical in a way, a grown man wrestling two dogs over a bright colored bag in the middle of the forest, the two hunters looked on with mirth for a moment then decided to step in.

"Paco!" shouted the big man. "Ram dog!" But it was no use, once latched onto fun sized prey, it took something more than a stern warning to get them to let loose, and the big man reached over and slapped them both lightly on the ends of their noses with a soft 'whack!", they yelped in mock pain, and ran away.

"Dang dogs, sorry mister," said the big man

and helped the big haole to his feet.

"That's okay," said Chris, as he looked at the felt bag. The dogs had torn two small holes in the bottom but it was still intact. He could see the gold wrapped present inside with teeth marks on the corners. It still looked good.

"What are you doing up here anyways?" the big man asked. He was obviously in charge while the small man kept silent. "These are hunting grounds, well-marked. You could have gotten hurt, or worse."

"Looking for Bull, Leilani, and Kainani. I heard they came hunting with you."

"Who told you that?"

"Auntie Tia, up on the north shore told me how to find your house, and then a small boy down by your house told me to look for you up here. Maybe he's your son? He seemed pretty sad not to be up here on the hunt."

The big man laughed. "That's Caleb, and yes, he's my son. Bull and the girls came up here with us it's true. But just to the start of the trail, not any farther. Hunting is dangerous as you can see, and Kainani is much too young."

"So you're the big haole looking for Bull!" exclaimed the small man as he slapped his own thigh. "We heard you might be heading this way."

"So I missed him?"

"By at least an hour maybe more. He's on his family vacation, holo-holo," said the big man.

"Looking around," said Chris with a sigh, heart sinking, visibly deflated. Then he cheered up quickly with a smile. Life was an adventure every moment and this was certainly turning into an interesting time. "You wouldn't be able to tell me where they're going next would you?"

"So, you're a friend?" asked the big man. Perhaps a bit wary, circumstances being strange as they were.

"Friend of a friend," said Chris. "From Alaska delivering a present, just got here a day too late. But I made a promise to deliver it, so here I am."

The big man nodded. Bull could take care of himself, that was not in question. And if someone was going to great lengths to deliver a present, all the better.

"He went down to Uncle Tommy's taro farm, it's in Waimanalo, about ten miles south from here. Turn right at the old store, then left at the big mango tree. You can't miss it."

Chris nodded; he was beginning to get the hang of directions on the island.

12.

Just as he was instructed Chris took a left at the big mango tree and went down the dirt road for a quarter mile, his view obscured by tall grass on either side of the road, a lime green corridor, then a clearing up ahead, and there on the left lay the taro fields just as Sean said.

There was an older model blue truck parked next to the side of one of the taro fields, the truck was big and boxy shaped with large buckets in the bed, and a big black dog busy barking at Chris as he drove slowly towards it.

The dog quickly closed the distance between them and circled the car, Chris kept the windows up as a precaution. It was a black Labrador retriever seemingly smiling as it was barking, tail wagging vigorously behind it like a hairy propeller driving the dog forward. It looked like a well-fed big dog, probably in the later part of its life. This was not an angry dog; it was a happy mongrel glad to see someone that might be bringing some food.

Still, Chris got out of the car carefully and surrendered to the jumping and attempts to lick at his face. Like a boxer in the ring with a formidable foe, Chris held off the feints and jabs of slobbery jowls and sharp claws on the ends of muddy paws until the dog got weary of trying and ran off to the side still barking while looking at the man in the middle of the taro field who was seemingly oblivious to all the action.

Chris marveled at the taro field, it was the first he'd ever seen in person, having only read about them in books and on-line. This particular one looked well kept. It was just about the size of a hockey rink, rectangle in shape, the edges raised banks. Half of the field was filled with a thin layer of water and looked as though it had just been cleared, bits and pieces of leaves and stems scattered about on the surface. While the other half was packed with a short plant that looked like bright green elephant ears the size of books set aloft by stems about a foot or two high rising out of the water.

The man was in the middle of this field, his back to the cleared part and was working steadily on the growing part, up to his knees in water and mud, pulling the taro one by one and putting the plant neatly into a little one-man skiff, an aluminum flat bottomed boat.

The dog just kept barking and barking, but still the man worked away, seemingly oblivious the commotion.

Chris put two fingers in the side of his mouth and whistled loudly towards the man. The dog seemed startled and sat down quickly, panting and out of breath. The man finally relented for his task and as he put another taro into the boat, stood tall and looked around at the source of the whistle.

Chris waved, and the man waved back, shrugged his shoulders, turned, and went back to work.

There was nothing left to do, thought Chris. He was too far away to yell a question and expect a reply. Into the patch he must go.

Off with the shoes, then the socks, and tossed into the car for safe keeping from the dog, he waded into the cool water, sinking first toes then full feet, ankles, and legs into the muck.

It was soft and gooey, with some fine pebbles here and there, soil well-worn perhaps over the ages broken down and liquefied over eons of time. He took a test step and needed to lift his foot straight out of the mud to move forward, then straight back into the sludge.

The aromatic aroma of fresh plant matter, a vegetable farm filled his nostrils and no mud had ever seemed cleaner in a way. He took another step and looked back at the dog that was sitting contently on the bank looking at him.

"Are you coming?" Chris asked it, but it just stood up and wagged its tail but stayed put.

Ever so slowly, step at a time Chris got closer to the center of the field. It was quite a workout, and as he got closer to the harvest realized that the small yacht filled with taro would need to be dragged across the pond to the edge, no small feat. The man hard at work looked very strong, short dark hair, arms thick, ropes of muscles on the back of his sweat covered neck.

Chris stopped next to the skiff, the man looked up with a genuine inquiring look on his face, as though surprised that someone had joined him in his quest to clear the field.

"Hello Tommy, your cousin Sean told me I could find you here."

The man didn't reply and Chris wondered if he could even hear the sound of words, or understand what he was saying, so he continued.

"I'm trying to find your other cousin Bull."

"Yes," the man said in perfect English. "I heard you might be coming. First work and then talk."

He went back to pulling at the taro. With both hands he reached down under the surface of the water, grasped the base of the stems and pulled, a slow sucking sound as the root lifted free, about the size of a softball covered in mud with feeder roots spreading from its surface, placing it carefully in big round buckets spaced evenly in the skiff that was now only a quarter of the way full.

Work first, then talk, thought Chris. It was a good motto as far as he was concerned and no stranger nor opponent to hard work decided to get at it.

He grabbed the rope at the front of the skiff and dragged it forward to give him room so they could work together. Dang, he thought it's heavy, he almost grunted with the effort but didn't want to let on that he was struggling and kept silent.

He watched the big man for a few moments, as he pulled the taro, and confident of the technique, gave it a try. He pulled his first taro, it tried to stay put at first but with some coaxing came free, a root the size of his fist, placed in the skiff, then bending back down for one more.

It was serene, they worked quietly. Every now and then the dog barked for no reason it seemed and after a while Chris stopped looking to see to why just like the big Hawaiian.

Birds in the distance sang sweet songs, melodies in a language that only they understood, every now and then a rooster cock a doodling, a random bark, as the trade winds steadily blew through the tall trees nearby and rustled the taro leaves, gently fluttering, tiny green sails set in place over a calm mud sea.

Bending over in that mud up to the middle of his shins, Chris forgot why he was even there in the first place, concentrating only on the task at hand, pulling taro after taro, within half an hour the skiff was full.

"All pau," said the big man. "We go."

He grabbed onto one of the ropes tied onto the front of the boat and handed the other to Chris and they trudged for the far bank with the dog trying to wag the tail off its rear end, barking and yelping in glee. Trudging like two human water buffalos pulling the skiff that Chris estimated must weigh in at more than five hundred pounds, buoyed by the muddy water that did not seem to float the boat much at all.

Finally at the bank, they lifted each of the buckets onto the bank.

"You're a good worker, I'll hire you if you want."

Chris chuckled. His legs and arms covered in a slim coating of mud.

"You know, that was actually pretty fun in a way. I wasn't thinking about anything else in the world for that short time except pulling the taro. It was almost like being in a trance. But I'm not looking for a job."

"What are you looking for?"

"For your cousin Bull."

"That's what I thought. He said you might be coming this way."

"You knew this whole time?"

"Of course. He said a big haole was looking for him. You're the only big haole I've seen today."

"Thanks," said Chris with a slight frown.

"But hey, cheer up my friend. This was kind of a test and you passed with flying colors."

"This was a test?"

"I knew you wanted me to tell you where he went, but that aint gonna happen unless I know for sure you're for real."

"I'm just trying to deliver a Christmas present. It's not a big deal." Not to anyone else, thought Chris, but it was becoming a bigger deal with every missed opportunity. He was worried that something might happen to the present before he could get it delivered and he'd have to go back to the North Pole and make another.

"You know I gotta tell you, Bull said a big haole was looking for him, but after seeing you pull that taro, I think you must be part Hawaiian."

He stuck out his hand and they shook bruddah bruddah style.

"Okay, so where do I go now?"

"Kalaupapa."

"Where's that, some little town next to Waikiki?" asked Chris hopefully. He was hungry and tired and wanted to lay down in a comfy hotel bed with the air-conditioner on full arctic blast.

Tommy laughed. "Waikiki? Naw brah, it's on a whole 'nother island, Molokai!"

"Molokai!" Chris shouted. He had a working knowledge of the islands, there were six major islands in the chain, Oahu, Big Island, Kauai, Maui, Lanai, and Molokai which was just to the east of Oahu, forty miles away.

Alright, he frowned for a moment then nodded. Okay, game on.

Tommy chuckled as he watched Chris' reaction.

"Don't worry, he's gonna be there for about three days, so all you gotta do is get over there and hook up. Shouldn't be too hard to find him either since there's only about fifty people there."

"That's all? Fifty people?"

"I don't mean on the whole island, just

Kalaupapa."

"Okay."

Chris didn't seem impressed.

"You don't know about that place, do you?"

"Not really."

"It's the old leper colony. Sort of a black eye, a disgrace for us in Hawaii. Bad times when that disease came to the islands. Wiped out a lot of families. Back in the eighteen hundreds, to around nineteen sixty, if you got leprosy, you were sent to Kalaupapa. It's a peninsula on the northwest portion on Molokai. Secluded, protected by a jagged coastline on one side, and steep cliffs on the other. Protected like a prison. Back in the old days, when you got sent there, you didn't come back."

Chris grimaced.

"Yeah, kids, parents, grandparents, whoever was diagnosed was forcibly taken from their families, from their homes, never to return. Anyways, those days are long gone but there's still a few patients left. The disease was cured back in the sixties and everyone was free to go finally. So, you got some kids from about that time, who were sent there, and now they're in their seventies and eighties, and the deal is, if they were sent there at any time, they can go back and live for free in one of the houses. Most of the people never wanted to go anywhere near that place again, and just like a prison when they got out, they stayed out. But it's a beautiful place, good fishing, good hunting, tropical landscape, trade winds, brah it's Hawaii nei, and some people like the seclusion.

Our uncle Joe lives there. He's a survivor, sent to the prison when he was just seven years old. Now he's eighty-nine, and still full of piss and vinegar as our grandma used to say. That's where Bull's at with Leilani and Kainani. It's the last leg of his trip. He's been going there for about twenty years now at exactly this time of the year, before he got married and before Kainani. It was a prison at one time, but now it's sort of a sacred place."

It was starting to get dark, the sun well on the other side of the island.

"I better get going," said Chris.

"Hey, you hungry?"

That stopped him in his tracks.

"What do you have?"

"Got a big bag of poi."

"The stuff we were just pulling?

"That's taro. We cook the root for a few hours and mash it with water. You never had poi have you?"

Chris shook his head, and Tommy smiled. He pulled out a bowl and spoon and filled it up with the sticky grey purplish goo, squeezing it out of the bag and handed the bowl to Chris who just looked at it.

"Looks like pudding."

"Taste it."

Chris shrugged his shoulders, scooped a big spoonful, and shoved it in his mouth which instantly became immobile. He winced, glomped, gulped and managed with great effort to get it all down.

"Tastes like paste."

"I wanted you to get the pure taste first. Now try it with this, eat a chunk of this then take a smaller bite of poi."

"What's this? Chris sniffed at the light brown stick he was handed.

"Smoked marlin, try it."

Chris did as he was told, took a bite of the marlin, then the poi and his face lit up. "Hey this is good."

Tommy handed him the bag of poi, and a zip lock with more marlin.

"You come work for me anytime, and I'll pay you good money, *and* give you good food."

13.

The small passenger plane lifted off the runway near the end of the reef and headed south into the trade winds. The double propeller gas turbine engines seemingly maxing out in power, wings buoyed by gusts, buffeted as they climbed slowly, methodically, out over the blue turquoise waters. They could see the two pilots in the cabin in front working the controls, one of the great things about flying on an ultra-small airliner, you see all the action.

Kainani had the window seat on the left, flanked by her dad Bull, and her mom had the window seat on the other side that would come in handy later in the flight when they flew by the north coast of Molokai. She held her dad's hand tight and told him not to worry since it was well known in their family that even though he was one of the toughest beach boys in the islands, he was deathly afraid of flying.

This was the most exciting part of their family vacation. They were headed to Kalaupapa on the secluded northeast corner of Molokai. It was off-limits to the general public;

you couldn't just go there whenever you wanted. You had to be invited, either to work for the parks department who controlled it, or as a guest of one of the residents, and there were very few of them left now.

Children, visitors under the age of sixteen weren't allowed. The leprosy patients, all throughout the years, weren't allowed to have children of their own, it was for the children's safety and try as they might for sterility among the population, whenever a new baby was born, those babies were taken away from their mothers at birth.

Those were terrible times.

For a child to visit the peninsula in the modern era needed special permission, one of the residents needed to make an official request and they weren't allowed to visit any of the areas that a former patient might frequent as it might bring back memories of great sadness.

Bull's great uncle Joseph was one of the residents, and not by his own choice.

In the year nineteen forty -seven, someone noticed a strange splotch on his skin, he was diagnosed with Hanson's disease, and was forcibly removed from his family and relocated to the infamous leper colony at Kalaupapa. In essence he was sentenced to imprisonment and certain death at the tender age of seven years old.

And yet as fate would have it, Joseph survived, a cure was discovered, and in nineteen sixty-nine when he was twenty-nine years old, he was released into the world, and he made the most of it, becoming a merchant marine and traveling the world, to every corner he could manage.

And when he reached his mid-seventies, his life forces slowing down, he returned to Kalaupapa to live out the remaining years of his life.

14.

There were two airlines that flew to the Kalaupapa peninsula on Molokai, and they were set off from the main terminal, over a mile away. Their fleet consisted of single and double prop planes that could handle the small runway.

When Chris got to the terminal, one of the desks was shut down, empty, the lights off, and the other was in the process. It didn't look promising.

"Yes sir, can we help you?" asked the pleasant young attendant.

"Yes, I'd like to go to Kalaupapa."

"Tomorrow or the next day?" asked the attendant hopefully.

"Not tonight I take it?"

"The last flight just left."

Chris winced.

"Do you have your permit?" she asked.

"What do you mean?"

"To go to Kalaupapa."

"I need a permit?"

"We can't board passengers without the official permit to enter the peninsula. You have to be sponsored by one of the residents or have official business with the state."

"You gotta be kidding me."

She handed him a sheet of paper, and there it was in black and white:

Exhibit A – Application for a Visitor Permit with lines for a sponsor's name.

"We couldn't have let you board the plane anyways without a permit."

Chris shook his head. Rules were rules.

"Now what am I going to do."

He took the paper, folded it up and walked away from the counter.

A janitor sweeping the floor nearby had been listening in on the conversation, he could hear bits and pieces of what was being said and knew the problem well.

"Psst," he whispered, and motioned with his head for Chris to come closer, then as Chris got within arm's length, he moved farther away so the attendant at the counter couldn't hear what he was saying.

He huddled conspiratorially with Chris, turning his back to the counter, shielding them from watching eyes.

"So, you want to go to Kalaupapa eh?"

Chris narrowed his eyes. "What, are you going to smuggle me in there for a price?"

The janitor feigned a shocked look.

"Because if that's what you're offering, I'm in," said Chris. "I need to get there no matter what."

The janitor smiled, missing a couple of teeth here and there, the grin was legitimate, he was genuinely happy with that response.

"You see," he whispered. "I could tell you were a man of wisdom. I could see it in your eyes. Sure, there's laws, and more laws. Some well-intentioned and right to have. But when you got laws that keep a man out of a place, for no good reason, I call that tyranny. Like we have a dictator running the place, ordering you what you can and can't do. Despots and rulers with rules." He whispered even quieter. "There's ways around rulers and the rules that they make."

Chris could tell what was what.

"You can't get a permit and go in there either, can you?"

He shook his head. "No, I had some run-ins with the park's rangers in the past, and now I'm banned for life. Officially that is."

He looked around to make sure no one was eaves dropping, then continued. "But I can still get in there whenever I want to, on my own terms."

"So, you'll take me there?"

He scoffed.

"No, I've gotta work. But I'll give you a tip."

"I'll take it," said Chris. "What are my options?"

"Well, you can take a boat across the channel, and swim in from just offshore."

Chris winced.

"But there's a quicker way. Take a plane."

Chris frowned.

"That's what I was trying to do."

"Not straight to Kalaupapa. You go topside,

then hike down the mountain."

"What's topside?"

"Every bit of dirt that's not Kalaupapa. Everything on the other side of the pali, the cliff that guards it like a sentry. You fly into the airport on top of the island, then catch a ride, or walk to the trail head, it's not far, but you don't take the trail. You gotta be smarter than that."

He tapped on his head with two fingers.

"You have to watch out for the rangers, they're tricky bastards. They have cameras all over the place. They act like they're protecting a top-secret military installation for crying out loud."

"Sounds like you know the place well."

He shrugged his shoulders.

"I grew up there, now I live over here."

"You're a bit of a rebel, aren't you?"

"Reformed. I just didn't like laws that kept me out of nature. Rules just to go fishing or surfing, or hunt shells wherever and whenever I wanted."

Chris went back to the counter.

"When's your next flight to Molokai, topside?"

The attendant looked at the janitor while shaking her head. He just smiled, and she double checked the list.

"Six thirty tomorrow morning."

Chris winked at the janitor as he passed. He could see the look in his eye.

"Thanks for the tip. You ever go to Vegas?"

"You kidding me? I work for the airport. I fly

for free. I don't do much gambling, it's boring, pulling the bandits arm and watching the wheels go around and around. I go to load up on the buffets. Shrimp and king crab all day long. I'm kind of like a camel in a way. I eat for two days, then I come back here and live off my hump."

Chris laughed and handed him a ten-dollar casino chip.

"I heard these are good for the buffets."

The janitor squinted at Chris while squeezing the chip tight

"What I'm really thinking about is going back to Kalaupapa. You got me fired up."

"Don't get caught," said Chris as he walked towards the parking lot.

He'd gone about twenty feet when he heard a shout from behind him.

"You either!"

How many times had he flown into countries off-limits. Totalitarian states, with dictators, iron regimes, no fun or wishful thinking allowed. How many times had his ancestors, from Chris the first to himself landed on rooftops in violation to deliver simple gifts to innocent children? Maybe to the children of prisoners, or of the dictators themselves?

No. He wouldn't get caught.

15.

By the time Chris got back to the hotel room it was well past nine, and Melissa was nestled deep under the blankets, the air conditioner on high, it felt great. He patted her gently to let her know he was there. She lifted her head from the pillow to look at him, face sunburned a bit puffy but happy and content.

He'd woken her up from a deep sleep and she looked a little disoriented.

"Did you deliver the present?" she mumbled.

"Not yet, but I'm getting closer. You wouldn't believe the places I went today." He got ready to sit down on the edge of the bed so he could tell her all about the wild adventures, then noted the sleepy nature of her eyelids drooping and heavy, barely holding them open and he smiled.

"Tomorrow, I'll tell you tomorrow."

Patted her on the head again and gently tucked the blanket under her chin. She settled back with a sigh, curled up and was back asleep in mere seconds.

He took the laptop and headphones out onto the balcony and got to work. Something important that he needed to do. Learning languages was second nature to him in a way. When growing up he learned ten new languages every year, it was required in his house with Santa Claus as his dad, who prided himself on knowing enough of each language to get by in a pinch.

They got easier the more of them that you learned, since they overlapped in many ways. Latin, Greek, and Germanic languages covered most of Europe, the African languages were similar once you learned Swahili. Chinese, Korean and Japanese interlocked once you caught onto the code and transcended into the southern Asian regions and into Polynesia. The lexical similarity of Tahitian to Hawaiian was about seventy five percent he read, and so he started there, he had a smattering knowledge of Tahitian, so he did a refresher course quickly, ten minutes listening to a story he knew well in many other languages. It was the same story and when you knew it word by word phrase by phrase, it became a Rosetta stone in a way in his mind, he could see the words, visualize the meaning.

Ten minutes of Tahitian and then twenty minutes of Hawaiian, it was fascinating, this sub set of a language developed and honed by a group of highly intelligent people isolated on these islands for thousands of years, their traditions and history was all oral, nothing in writing, and if it wasn't for the missionaries ironically, who began writing the stories and transcribing the language bit by bit into words, it might have been lost forever.

He looked past the curtain to the digital clock on the desk. Ten o'clock. Time for sleep. By six o'clock and before dawn he'd be on a plane bound for Molokai, and he'd better be well rested. If the past day was any indication, he could be in for another roller coaster adventure tomorrow and he'd better be ready.

16.

The next morning Chris got to the airport early. He left the hotel well before dawn and left a note on the nightstand:

'Heading to Molokai, will be back later – C.C.'

It was a small single engine plane with four single seats on each side of the aisle and one bench seat at the back.

Since it was a such a small plane, every bag and passenger had to get weighed so they could even out the displacement.

Chris got on the baggage scale and the attendant didn't bat an eyelid as she wrote down the number. He looked at the digital read-out. Three hundred ten pounds. He gained five pounds and barely ate anything since he'd been on the island. He counted on his thumb and forefinger the only two meals of late, nodding his head knowingly.

"Auntie Tia's portagee soup, and Uncle Tommy's fish and poi."

The plane ride was quick. Once they were in the air it was a thirty-five-minute flight. Chris sat in the middle of the bench seat at the back completely at ease. The cockpit door was open and the passengers could all see the pilot and co-pilot working at the controls.

It was fun to bump around up in the trade wind clouds, without having to do anything except watch, no hands on the reigns, no shouting out 'on Dasher on Dancer', and when they finally came down on the black asphalt tarmac in the middle of Molokai, Chris chuckled to himself. Just a couple of nights ago he'd made a few thousand landings on rooftops around the globe, and only two were that bumpy. Oldenburg and Paramus.

From the map it looked like it was about eight miles to the trail, and he decided to just hoof it and see what might happen on this little island.

Walking next to the road for a few minutes, a pickup truck pulled up next to him. The front was filled with packages, and the back with yelping dogs.

"Where are you heading sir, down to Kaunakakai?" asked the young local man at the wheel.

"Kalaupapa."

He tilted his head, not the answer he expected.

"Down the trail?"

"Yup, unless there's a better way."

"You could take a plane." He motioned with his thumb back to the airport.

"I missed my chance. Walking's my only option."

"Do you have a permit?"

"Are you a park ranger?"

"Naw, I'm just a delivery guy. I pick up packages for the local pharmacy."

"I don't have a permit."

The driver nodded as it all became clearer. He was a rebel.

"Hop in, I'll take you to the trail head. It's about eight miles from here. I'm Josh."

There was no room in the front of the truck so Chris rode in the back with the dogs, all five of them running from one side to the other when they thought they spotted some type of animal, or an enemy dog from an opposing camp in another truck or the side of the road.

They always gave special note to any truck, as that seemed to be the hiding place of all their furry foes.

Finally, the truck stopped, and although the dogs whimpered and pleaded, their master was firm and they stayed put, while Chris was free to go and hopped out the back. The dogs looked at him eagerly waiting for him to perhaps give the golden command to jump out, but from the front of the truck came the simple firm command that was the law:

"Stay!"

Josh got out and commanded them all to sit which they did, barely containing themselves after the long, exciting ride, sitting on tails that nearly wagged them right over the side rails of the truck.

Finally, content that his commands were clearly met he let down the tailgate, the unspoken instruction, and they all scampered out running to the nearest bushes, their business at hand to sniff and mark territory, number one on the list.

"Well good luck," said Josh. "I hope the rangers don't catch you. They don't mess around. They've got cameras all over the place you know."

"On the trail."

"Yeah, on the trail, and scattered around in the forest. Motion detected I heard."

"What could they do with me if they catch me?"

"Write you a ticket."

Chris scoffed.

"Or throw you in jail."

That gave Chris pause, but there was no way around it.

"Thanks for the ride." He called out to the dogs and they circled around him yapping and trying to lick his face. Chris was too quick for them and gave each of them a playful wrestle and release, then waved to Josh as he walked to the start of the trail.

Right there on a tree down to the right, camouflaged like bark was a small camera, no doubt about it. Chris frowned and walked straight past it, whistling as he went, and around the first bend decided to make a break for it. No stranger to the wilderness, and forests in particular it should be an easy feat he figured. Into the thick brush he went and down the hill.

After a few hundred yards of plodding and pushing through ferns and thick brush he came to a small clearing where he could sit down and gather himself, he needed to catch his breath.

At the top of the pali, two thousand feet high his small clearing faced straight north, and he looked out over the peninsula spread out below him. It was a generally flat plane with minimal bumps and hills, perhaps laid out from an ancient lava flow in the distant past.

It was funny, in a way, the peninsula looked like the shape of an elf's hat rounded at the bottom and standing tall at the top with a slight point.

The small town what there was of it was on the left side of the elf's hat, bordering the roughhewn rocky shoreline and spread out in a semi-circle only taking up a small fraction of the peninsula, perhaps less than of one hundredth of the entire area. Houses spaced evenly apart, streets at square angles to each other, he counted twenty blocks, and estimated a hundred houses, no more. Some bigger buildings down by the small port and the airport off towards the north set apart from the town.

Sitting there in silence made him reflect on the whole family business, and his own life in general. They'd had a good run, the Claussen's, aka Santa Claus. Hundreds of years, caring for the magic along with the elves, but nothing lasts forever. Without an heir to take his place, the magic of Christmas, as far as a real Santa Claus delivering toys was concerned, would be over.

Sure, there would be dads, and performers

wearing costumes, acting the part, maybe it would be enough. He wondered about the elves, those magical beings, what would become of *them*? Would they just fade off into one of their gold, or diamond mines and slowly forget the fine talent of making toys?

He sighed mightily, better not to think depressing thoughts this far out in the wilderness. Surrounded by nature created by the ultimate magical hand, the troubles of an heirless Santa were microscopic in comparison.

He was a peanut, less than that even, a speck of sand, a microbe in the vastness of the great universe. He had a job to do, nothing more, a cog in the great wheel of restoration, recompense.

They still had time left after all. He was only in the beginning of his fortieth decade of life, and Mrs. Claus was right there with him. His parents had *him* when they were just south of forty so he was only technically late in the game by a few years.

Having a child though, was not as easy as ordering one up like an item on the menu, having the waitress deliver it to the table, a gift on the list and having the elves manufacture it to spec.

A child was perhaps the greatest miracle of them all and the vast wilderness, all this great planet, the universe, all creation would be void without them.

As Chris sat there studying the small town, he wondered if his own dad, or grandfather, or any of his Santa Claus ancestors down the line had ever delivered a present there. He knew for a fact that he never had. And it made sense in a way, with the history of the place. The last time a child had lived there was over sixty years ago.

Long before his time.

Speaking of which, he reminded himself as he shouldered the small red sack and stood up, he had a job to do, so he'd better get down the hill and get it done.

The split second that he stood up, he stood still, senses keenly alert.

Now Chris didn't know much about pigs, not many species of them traversed the artic regions, but he was expert as far as deer were concerned. Reindeer especially, but all deer large and small had similar qualities and mannerisms.

He could tell, without a doubt that there were deer nearby. He crept slowly forward.

He couldn't see them, but he could hear them rustling around in the bushes, he could smell them, their hide a distinct rancid odor much like cattle and horses, and last of all he nearly stepped in one of their deposits on the ground.

They were close.

He quieted his footsteps, like an Indian hunter pushing the branches to the side silently stalking his prey. There, up ahead, three does, gently grazing, nibbling grass next to a large stump of an old fallen tree.

They were Axis deer, not as large as reindeer, but just as athletic, able to leap ten feet in the air from a standing stop. First one then the others lifted their heads smelling the air, sensing danger, but Chris was downwind and he kept his head still, studying them, surrounded by thick brush, only his eyes peering out.

They were a light tan with white spots on their flanks, around a hundred pounds not more. Then from around the corner of the fallen tree came the buck. Magnificent in shape and size, nearly twice as large as the does, dark brown nearly black, two hundred, maybe two fifty, rippled flanks, and on top of his head a rack with ten points. Sharpened horns, ready for battle. A champion. He was all business, not nibbling at the grass but keeping watch, the guardian of his brood, his worry, his clutch.

Black nose sniffing, black eyes like coal searching, then latching onto Chris's eyes, staring straight at him, somehow pinpointing with precision, eons of survival skills honed sharp and true, perhaps the sunlight glinting off Chris eyes. Or the strange color of the iris blue. He tried to shut them to mere slits, squinting at the beast but it was no use. The bull deer walked slowly forward.

Wild animals in general, and deer in particular are primarily interested in being left alone, and given the options mostly choose flight. There are occasions, and this trait is also evident in humans, when they sense their backs against the wall, or with family nearby needing protection, choose fight.

Such was the case at this very instant, Chris knew, and he tried to silently back away into the bushes. When he had gone a couple of feet not more, he turned and began to run crashing through hanging branches, clumps of leaves while behind him he heard the snorting of the beast. Whether it be a horse, or a bison, or a bull, or a deer when they put their head down and charged, you got out of the way.

Chris ran.

Out into the open, he should have been able to put some distance between them, and usually a buck would quit the chase if there was no imminent danger, but this buck kept galloping behind, maybe something about Chris pissed him off. Maybe it was the red sack over his shoulder. Or maybe because he lived with a herd of reindeer all year every day of his life, riding them feeding them, brushing them, that some essence of their scent had seeped into his pores, and to this crazed buck deer Chris was a rival, an enemy, a foe.

The edge of a small cliff got in the way of their path, and as Chris teetered on the edge looking back in dread, the buck lowered its sharp rack, while putting on hoof brakes, then with a flick of his head lifted Chris in the air flinging him over the edge and down the cliff.

He landed hard once and rolled twice coming to rest against a boulder that stopped against his stomach. He winced for a moment expecting some type of pain, but all was well and as he looked back up the hill through the cloud of dust, the buck snorted, stomped one front hoof, and turned to walk away.

"Yeah, you better get out of here!" Chris

shouted. "You better hope Donner and Blitzen don't hear about this. They'll fly down here and kick your ass!"

The buck looked back once with one coal black sinister eye and Chris decided to shut up and get the heck out of there.

He scampered to his feet, slung the red bag over his shoulder, climbed over the boulder and disappeared into the jungle.

17.

Meanwhile, down in Kalaupapa, Kainani and her family were having the time of their lives. Residing in Waikiki was big city life. There was constant commotion, and noise. Here it was quiet country living at its finest.

When the little plane touched down the day before, there were three people waiting near the terminal which was the size of a large house.

As they got in the car, Bull had forgotten the protocol, and started to put on his seatbelt, the law of the land, state law that was, ingrained in his actions.

"What are you doing?" asked his uncle with a stern look. "You know where you're at? This is Kalaupapa."

"Oh, right, sorry uncle," said Bull cheeks turning red. "I forgot." As he put the seatbelt on the side.

Kalaupapa was like the wild west, no rules when you were driving your car. You didn't need a license, didn't need a license plate, and you definitely didn't need to wear a seatbelt.

The residents, especially the older ones,

considered it a weakness, and scoffed at anyone who wore one. They were on their own over here on the peninsula. There weren't any police. Not wearing a seatbelt was a sign of independence in a way, a small symbol of anarchy, rebellion.

They were renegades to be sent here and renegades they remained. It was like a badge of honor that no one could take away. And make no mistake about it, the older residents, the survivors of leprosy, and the cruel banishment to this place considered themselves rebels. To most of them, it was the real reason they survived.

The only law in town were the park rangers and they had no real jurisdiction over the residents.

They were in place mostly to keep the outsiders out, and maintain the buildings that were steadily falling apart, until one day when the last of the survivors passed away, and the peninsula transferred back to the state.

As long as there was a single survivor living at Kalaupapa, it was off-limits to the general population. No willy nilly travel looky loos permitted unless you were invited by one of the residents or had business with the state.

There was a struggle for power among two different camps.

One wanted to keep it as is. Pristine and empty, or only with limited paying guests in the buildings that remained standing.

While the other camp wanted a small hotel, condos, restaurants, and tours all around the area. For the taxes of course.

Uncle Joseph stopped at the little store and turned to Kainani.

"Do you want an ice cream cone?"

She nodded with a smile and they all got out. They were on the main street of the town, a wide boulevard with sidewalks. Two of the churches were nearby, and across the street was the little harbor, empty of boats. In fact, the entire street stretching off into the distance both ways was completely empty. As though they were the only people left in the world.

Uncle Joseph led the way through the double doors and the man at the counter looked from the newspaper he was reading and smiled.

"Hi Joseph."

"This is my family from Oahu, you might remember them from last year."

"Yes, I do, welcome back."

"Bully, his wife Leilani, and Kainani."

The man stood up and shook all their hands and gave a fist bump to Kainani.

"You were just this big last year," said the man motioning with his hand below Kainani's shoulder.

"We're just here for ice cream," said Joseph and motioned Kainani to the freezer. "Pick out one for each of us."

"So," asked Joseph, leaning on his cane. "Have you seen the new marine biologist?"

The man nodded. Every year or so they rotated the park rangers and scientists to new locations, it was like being in the military, they wanted to expand each individual's capacity and knowledge in different areas, it was a method to prevent complacency, to avoid stagnation. A rolling stone etc. The new marine biologist was about twenty-five or six, a vivacious brunette who dressed sharply and cut a nice figure.

"Have you seen her?" asked Joseph again.

"Yeah, I saw her," said the young man.

"She's mine," said Joseph with a smile. "Stay away from her."

Bull and Leilani tried to hold back their giggles. Uncle Joseph was nearly ninety years old and cantankerous as ever.

The young man began to blush, not sure what to say.

Joseph chuckled. "Hey, I was just kidding."

They sat on the bench outside the store in the shade and watched the empty street. An orange cat ran from the harbor towards the church.

"Father Patrick's cat," said Uncle Joseph. "Bailey. Must have been looking for some fish."

A small dust cloud kicked up from the swirling trade winds and that was about all the action in the town. That was it.

A cat and some dust.

They finished their ice cream and piled back in the car, Bull remembered not to buckle up and they travelled up the road, past the seaside pavilion looking over the harbor, the visitors' dormitories on the right, the flagpole, and the state parks office, then on the left, the small infirmary, and hospital. Joseph glanced over then kept his eyes straight as they passed.

"It's a good thing they have the hospital right there," said Bull. "In case you need it."

Joseph shook his head. "I'll never go back there. I hope. Not till the end which is a long way away." He looked over at Bull and smiled. "A long way if I got anything to say about it."

They pulled into the driveway of the little house. It was tidy and clean, kept in good shape by the parks department and their staff, mowing the yard, trimming bushes, cleaning the windows, power washing and painting as needed.

The house was his to stay in as long he wanted.

Joseph was tired, and even though it was early in the day decided to take a nap before dinner.

The next day they took a ride around the perimeter of Kalawao County. The road if you could call it that was more like a path of round boulders with stream washouts here and there. The truck they rode in was hefty, their driver and tour guide worked for the parks department and it was his job to check on the area once a week. They didn't see a single other person or vehicle for the whole five-hour ride.

They stopped at the salt flats where the giant winter waves swept over black lava, then when it dried left pure rock salt in the small holes and bowls.

All was barren for a few miles, then they rounded the corner of the peninsula and were facing east over the ocean that bordered the sharp northern cliffs running east towards Maui and the Big Island. Here there was some sort of spring, fresh water that bubbled out of the aquifer from somewhere down below, pushed out here at the edge of island from the mountains at the center. There was a cave filled with lush green plants, seemingly alien in this barren landscape, fed by the fresh water. The mouth of the cave faced straight east with a wide view of the ocean.

"This was the lookout," said their guide. "Back in the ancient days. A select group of women set up camp here and manned it day and night throughout the year. They could survive here with the freshwater spring. If ever they saw a war party, canoes coming from Maui or the Big Island, they set off a bonfire with black smoke to warn the village.

They went inland again to a paved road heading farther east and passed the congregational church Siloama, then Saint Philomena, the church built by Father Damien.

Out to the very end of the road and took pictures looking down the northeast coast of Molokai, towering cliffs, and jungle covered pinnacles just offshore.

Back at the town Joseph took them all around. To orchards filled with fruits. The movie theatre, museum, the nun's home, and the old orphanage, it was empty, quiet, forlorn.

Joseph watched the old building carefully as though looking for old friends that might be walking around. Spirits of days long gone.

They drove all around the town without

seeing a single person then out past the last shack on the outskirts on the western edge of the peninsula and headed for the black sand beach past the bridge.

The sign on the end of the bridge said: 'No Mules Allowed'.

Out onto the black sand beach, gentle waves lapping against the smooth shore.

Into clear water they dove and swam while Joseph waited on the shore, no rocks or coral reef here, just smooth fine grains almost like a powder, soft on their feet and toes. But it was also a problem in a way since it stuck to your skin like dust. They sat on logs at the edge of the forest and wiped the sand off with towels, completely refreshed. The long empty coastline stretching off to the west.

"Hey, I got an idea," said Bull. "Let's go check out the trail that goes up topside."

"The trail's closed," said Joseph.

"Just a little ways uncle, not far, I want to see what it looks like."

18.

Down near the bottom of the cliff, Chris could see the end of the tunnel so to speak. The perilous route that he'd decided to journey was beginning to level out, he was almost safe but not quite yet. There was an especially steep little cliff that he needed to negotiate. He could go around it to the right or veer off to the left and jump back on the trail for the last few yards.

One part of him wanted to just get back on the trail, while the other told him to keep on the wayward path. He made it this far might as well keep with it till he was at the very bottom.

Two things happened at once.

He smelled a familiar scent on the breeze, the trade winds blowing from over the Pali swirling downwards in this particular stretch of the mountain. Swirling with the scent of deer and it seemed as though they must be located and travelling on the trail just to the left.

At that very moment in time that the scent appeared, a family of four walked around a bend in the trail, coming from below. The trail was muddy from the rain, and they seemed to be more concerned with not slipping than what was around them in the forest.

The father was in front, followed by a young girl who looked to be around seven or eight, then a woman who must be the mother and an old man bringing up the rear.

Now from above moving swiftly, the deer seemed to be spooked by something higher up on the trail and the sound of fast hooves filled the air.

"Run!" shouted Chris and pointed down the hill.

The group was startled and froze. Bull took one look at the strange man lurking in the bushes while realizing the potential source of the sound of hooves coming towards them.

Stampede.

He turned and grabbed Kainani, throwing her over his shoulder, Leilani cowered behind him, and although Bull thought about running it was no use. Uncle Joseph could barely walk, let alone run. He pulled his family behind him, and got ready to with-stand the onslaught, whatever might come.

Chris jumped down onto the trail and ran towards them.

They heard the distant sound of a gunshot, loud crack then an echo reverberating off the cliffs and throughout the valley. It was a hunter, high up on the hillside that spooked them.

The herd of deer led by the buck crashed out of the forest, blind with fear, running for their lives willing to mow down anything in their path to survive, and at that moment the little family of four were in the way.

From the side Chris sprinted fast, the fastest he'd ever run in his life, trying to hedge the big buck to the side, it looked at him with a single fierce eye, blazing and yet black, recognizing his enemy from the hillside, snorting with anger it tried to turn its head, but Chris was onto his game, and being on the side gave him an edge. He grabbed the sharp horn as it turned towards him with one hand, with the other latched onto the tuff behind the beast's head, and as the buck tried to fling him off with a toss of his head, Chris leaped onto its back.

The buck freaked out, shrieking with primordial fear as though a cougar had leaped onto its backside for the kill, it stopped mid leap and kicked back hooves in the air. With strong grip and sheer will, Chris twisted its horns as though he were driving a car and steered the buck away from the young family, pointing it instead back along the edge of the mountain and the thick forest. With a final heave, the buck jumped in the air with a pirouette, and Chris went flying off the back into a mud pit, and that was that. An ignominious end to a feat of bravery.

The stampede of hooves, crashing branches disappeared somewhere deep in the jungle and then all was suddenly quiet.

Chris pulled himself out of the mud pit, first standing as globs of wet leaves and branches intertwined with muck and grime fell off his backside, then walking gingerly to the dry grass.

He pulled a vine off his nose and ran a dirty hand over the nub of white hair, turning it brown. Most people would be fully and totally humiliated by this predicament, but he saw the humor as always, and chuckled, then the chuckle turned into a full bellied laugh, leaning over, hands on knees, laughing until he ran out of breath, then sighed deeply and turned to look at the spectators standing off to the side in a straight line.

Bull was at the front hands ready by his side, scared and yet angry face, his wife was directly behind him peering out from around his massive shoulders with a slight sheepish grin on her face, and Kainani was behind her mother also peering out from the side of her waist. Joseph behind her at the very back of the pack. Kainani was trying to hold back a giggle, the light in her eyes bright at the sight of the big man pulling himself out of the mud pit and yet still, somehow full of good humor. She wanted to go jump in the mud also to see how it felt and join in the fun but held herself back to see how this played out.

Bull pointed his finger suspiciously.

"Eh, I heard someone who looks like you been looking for us all over Hawaii-nei. Is that you?"

Chris nodded. He was hungry and tired and now sore "Yes, and it's been quite an adventure trying to find you."

Bull scrunched up his face as though he didn't understand what was being said, and

Chris re-grouped and pulled out his best pidgin for a re-try.

"I mean, I bin lookin' all ovah da place for you buggahs."

Bull waved his finger. "Eh brah, no pull out da pidgin, I understand what you're saying. The question is *why* are you trying to find us."

"It's a long story."

"Okay, we're waiting."

"I have a present for Kainani."

"For my daughter? Why?"

Bull's head tilted like an actual protective bull with horns that was getting ready to charge.

Chris sighed and shrugged his shoulders. He was tired and hungry and couldn't tell a lie.

"The present fell out of the bag somewhere in New Jersey, or maybe Oldenburg, I'm still not sure where, then it got stuck under the sleigh and I didn't find it till the day after Christmas."

"What bag, what sleigh? What da heck you talkin' about?"

Chris frowned.

"The bag with all the toys for all the good girls and boys. Riding on my magic sleigh with eight reindeer."

"You sure you didn't hit your head when you slid off that cliff?"

Realizing that there was no way to dance around this any longer, he decided to come clean so to speak.

"Look Mr. Kaupea, Bull, I know you all might not believe me, but after all I've been through, all *we've* been through. Well, I'm Santa Claus."

The look on all four of their faces turned different shapes of blank. Bull, eyes scrunched with incredulous dis-belief, Mrs. Kaupea with shocked eyes slightly alarmed, Uncle Joseph squinting through wrinkled eyelids, skeptical of practical jokes no matter how elaborate, and Kainani eyes wide open and mouth agape believing that it might somehow actually be true.

Then Bull took a deep breath and began laughing out loud, adrenaline shock of almost getting run over by a herd of deer, and now this. Overwhelmed he let loose. Big bellowing howls as he bent over slapping his thighs, the others behind decided it was okay to celebrate since dad wasn't worried, and they also started laughing at the crazy mud-covered man.

Then just as suddenly, Bull stopped laughing, his face turned serious and he said quite simply: "Enough playing around, you got any ID?" He cocked his head menacingly. "Santa?"

But Chris just shook his head. All he had was a credit card in his back pocket that said his name was Chris Claussen. He looked over at the box sticking out of the red bag, laying on the side of the mud pit, at one time not long ago it was brand new shiny gold paper wrapped Christmas present, and now it was smudged with dirt and mud, crumpled a bit on one corner, paper torn on one end, hoof marks, dog bites and all. He walked over and picked it up, tried to wipe some of the dirt off and straighten the crinkled paper.

"All I have is this present. This should be proof enough."

"A dirty box?"

"It's what's inside that matters," said Chris. "It's a present for Kainani. She wished for it, wished for it in secret with a heart as big as Christmas itself, and now I can finally deliver it and go home."

He handed it to Bull who held it in both hands, looking suspiciously at it like it was a bomb ready to explode, or had some kind of animal that would jump out. He shook it gently, then looked behind him.

"You wished for a present Kainani? Secretly? What you said at auntie Tia's was true?""

She nodded, eyes wide with wonder. Bull thought for a moment, a great momentous decision weighing heavily on him, to trust or not trust, in the middle of the forest on the north shore of Molokai, mere footsteps away from one of the most sacred places in Hawaii.

He made up his mind, and handed the box to Kainani, who looked down at the object in her hands, and up to the mud man, to her dad, Uncle Joseph, then her mom, all eyes were latched firmly on her.

"Well, open it," said her dad.

She decided to start with the torn piece on the end pulling a long swath of dirt covered gold paper with a crisp tearing sound, then all the rest of the paper came quickly off. It was a thin cardboard box, she opened it, and inside were the running shoes that she wished for, long ago, brand new and shining white with bright green edges and pink shoelaces. She checked the size on the inside by the heel.

Size nine. Perfect.

Now smiling wide from ear to ear, she knew that this big mud-covered man standing in front of them really was Santa Claus. She made that wish in secret and never told anyone what she wished for. Then she handed the shoes to her mom, who held them with wonder now on her face.

"Why are you giving them to me?"

"I wished them for you momma. Your feet are always tired when you come home from work. Look, they're size nine. That's your size, not mine."

Her mom reached down and hugged Kainani tight.

Now it was Santa's turn to have *his* face turn a certain shape of blank and he nodded his head while a smile slowly spread out on his big muddy face, for this right in front of him was the true meaning of Christmas.

"You wished for a present not for yourself, but for your mother who you love. That is perhaps the best gift of all. If that present hadn't fallen out of the bag and been delivered on Christmas Eve I never would have known."

He hesitated; how could this be possible but then knew it was true.

"So, I guess in a way this is a gift for me as well, to see it in person."

Chris took a step back to give himself room,

took a deep breath, made his back straight, and bellowed out:

"HO, HO, HO, MERRY CHRISTMAS!"

His giant muddy jelly belly jiggling as he shouted, the sound of his greeting bouncing off the jungle covered valley walls, echoing up into the sky and off into the distance.

Uncle Joseph however was still skeptical, and he picked up the gold wrapping paper that was laying on the ground, torn, stomped on, teeth marks and all, but still in one piece. He smelled it and tested the elasticity.

Chris was watching him carefully.

Joseph looked up from the paper now held carefully in both hands, the skepticism was gone and in its place on his old face was a tinge of sweet wonder, a glow, and Chris nodded his head, knowingly.

"You've seen that type of paper before."

"Yes," said Joseph. "A very long time ago when I first came to this place. I was about seven years old, The same age as Kainani. Torn from my family and placed in the orphanage with all the other boys. Oh, I didn't get the present, probably wasn't good enough to deserve it, none of us were, except for this one boy. He was the most frail of us all. He found the present with his name under the tree on Christmas morning and no one knew where it came from. The paper had a strong scent like pine, and the gold coating was heavy, as though it was real gold. Is it?"

The way that he asked the question proved that all doubt was gone from the old man. Chris smiled.

"Yes, the gold is real, not twenty-four carat, that's too soft, it's around twenty-two, and just a tiny bit of the stuff, a coating so thin that you'd need a hundred presents to melt a nugget the size of an eraser on the end of a pencil. The elves make the paper from pine trees harvested in Autumn when their sap is the strongest and the scent most intense, the gold from a mine under a deep snow-covered mountain. To the elves, the paper and box is every bit as important as the present inside, and they put the same effort into its creation."

"Yes," smiled Joseph. "Inside was a box much like this one, filled with sugar ginger cookies, the boy shared them with all of us, we each got a cookie, all fifty of us."

"What about the paper and the box?" asked Chris.

Joseph smiled. "We burned the box in the fireplace, we were cold. The box burned bright and hot but not the paper."

"Gold doesn't burn," said Chris.

"No, it seemed to sizzle and then melt, dripping down into the ash pit. The fire was welcome for a moment. Those were terrible times, but somehow that box of cookies gave us all hope, if only for the morning of that single day. You say that gold doesn't burn, and the elves make the paper?

"It's by design, they invented it back in the misty past. Gold doesn't burn, and so a present wrapped tight in pure gold doesn't burn, no matter how close to the fireplace that it's placed. They found out that pure gold no matter how thin was like a fireproof shield."

Chris studied Joseph.

"You say that the present was delivered when you were seven?"

"Eight two years ago. I remember it like it was yesterday. Wasn't it you that delivered it?"

Chris shook his head.

"That would have been my grandfather. I inherited the job from my father, his son."

Eighty-two years ago, thought Chris, his mind whirling, calculating.

"My grandfather would have been just about my age. Flying the sleigh and eight reindeer down onto the peninsula, onto the orphanage roof. Against all the quarantine rules. Breaking the law."

What strange events, like stars lining up in the sky brought him to this place, at this very moment in time. If he hadn't been here to deliver the present, also now breaking the law, would the buck deer have run the little family over?

They watched Chris carefully, it appeared that he might be about to say something of great importance. Something of utmost significance.

It was all suddenly too much for Chris. He smiled weakly; all emotion drained from his core.

"Merry Christmas," he whispered gently while bowing at the waist to them in honor.

Then he said simply: "And now I can go home."

He turned without another word and started walking towards the sunlight glinting through the trees from the West, back to the trail to go up topside.

Bull took one step forward and grabbed him by the arm with a strong grip

"Not so fast Santa. You aint leaving deeze islands till we give you a *real* local send-off. Since you're a true Hawaiian now, you're gonna get a true Hawaiian style aloha."

19.

Chris and Melissa walked down the pathway full of apprehension. Even though it was still early in the evening, not yet seven o'clock, the sunset was on its last light.

They could see Bull waiting at the gate for them, beaming widely from ear to ear with his wife Leilani on one side and Kainani on the other.

Bull gave them all a big bear hug, and then whispered in Chris' ear:

"Don't worry, it's still our little secret, no one knows you're Santa. As far as everyone knows, you're just a great friend from Alaska."

Behind them, in what looked like an arena were a dozen tables filled with over a hundred guests talking loudly, drinking, eating pupus and having a grand time.

Bull held up his hand, the crowd became silent and it was apparent that they were all waiting for the main guest's arrival since they all stood up and clapped.

All was silent for a moment then a young man dressed in a loin cloth held a conch shell up to his lips and blew an eerie sound, wavering in the air, a mournful horn, three times he blew the horn, a high note drifting to a low somber tone that lingered and disappeared.

A woman with long grey hair dressed in flowing white gown, pounding her open hand on a large double ended gourd began a chant in Hawaiian, drawing out the words long and full of melody. It was a blessing for the party, for the food, for the people.

It was a language that Chris understood now, and he whispered in Melissa's ear to translate. The spirits of the land, of the water and the air, from the four corners of the world, from ancient Tahiti far away, for the ancestors, for the living, for the yet to be born. The last word of her chant drifted in the night air like a mist heard not seen and disappeared.

Bull was still holding his hand in the air in salute and brought his hand down very slowly like a conductor starting a concert.

The drums started lightly with a rat-a-tat-tat wooden drumstick tapping against the edge of a simple piece of wood, a piercing high note, then the big deep booming bass drum beaten with the big stick rounding out the low side, then a medium sized drum kicked in with a staccato beat, filling with air with a grinding rhythmic cadence coming from the stage lit with flaming torches, the edges dressed with fresh cut fern and ti leaves flanked by tall kahili on each of the four corners, tall wooden staffs topped with yellow and red feathers.

As Bull relayed to Chris and Melissa, the

kahili was a standard, a symbol of the Aliʻi, the Chiefs, and signified power from the heavens.

In the ancient days, a kahili was made from the long bones of a rival enemy king and topped with feathers from birds of prey.

"Don't worry," he winked. "These are just wood. But the power they carry is still there."

Melissa expected half naked savages to jump out of the dark jungle surrounding them, and she was soon nearly correct. From the back of the stage streamed young men and women, dancing on the balls and heels of their feet as they walked to the pounding drums, knees, and elbows straight, then at odd angles, crouching, eyes wild, flaring nostrils, untamed hair, as though warriors ready to enter the fray.

The two lines met in the middle, the men with loin cloth and woven green ti leaves for their ankles and wrists, the women with the same plus tight fitting tops, and bright red and yellow flowers woven into their hair. They danced intense as the guests watched in awe, then as though they were one being with many arms and legs, feet together, hands in the air, eyes towards the heavens, dancers and drums gave one last mighty heave and as one stopped.

The crowd roared their approval and the party was off to fierce start.

Bull, Leilani, and Kainani led the way to the table for the guests of honor in front of the stage. Chris would have the head of the table with Melissa on his left. All of the tables were lined up facing the stage like spokes on a wheel so that everyone had a good view of the action.

The table itself was decorated like the stage with ferns and ti leaves, flowers, and shells, soft white lanterns, pitchers full of punch, bowls full of berries and nuts.

Everyone stopped by the table to say hello to the Claussen's. While everyone was a new face for Melissa, almost everyone was a new face for Chris, and a few that he'd seen the past few days. Benny from the chicken fights, Tia and her whole family from the north shore, Sean and his brother from the pig hunt, Tommy from the taro patch, even Uncle Joseph from Kalaupapa took a flight over, eighty-nine years old and still kicking it.

The luau buffet was full of every delicacy that the Hawaiians prized. Pork and poi, lomi salmon, and rice, sweet potato, cooked and raw fish of every shape and size, some fileted, and some crisply fried with their skin and head still intact, dried marlin and ahi, squid, opihi, urchins, green and red seaweed, sweet coconut haupia, heaps and piles that kept coming from the makeshift kitchen on the side, billowing with smoke.

When most all of the guests had their fill, Bull and Chris kept going, they paced themselves and were both in their own right, champions in the eating department, they eyed each other from the sides, knowing the bragging rights that were at stake, but it finally became apparent to both of them that this was a contest that no-one could win. Someone had to make a move.

"You know," said Bull with a great painful

sigh. "Us Hawaiians, we have a saying at a luau, that you don't stop eating when you're full. You stop eating when you're tired." He tried to burp but was much too packed to manage it. He pushed his chair a few inches from the table to give himself more room "We also have another saying. When you're finished, when you're done, when it's time to clock out from whatever you're doing whether it's at work or at play, you say 'all pau'."

Chris got the message, agreed with the unspoken acknowledgment of a truce, and pushed his chair back as well, waving the back of his hand at the last un-eaten bite and proclaimed gratefully.

"All pau."

They all laughed. Then around and around the table stories and jokes poured out, the whole embodiment of the luau like a lubricant oiling everyone's sharp wits and their tongues, the banter rolled like surf around an island ebbing and flowing in wave after wave.

Soon guests began to leave, and as the party began to wear down, Kainani yawned and leaned her cheek against her mother's soft shoulder, eyes closed.

"Well," said Leilani. "This has been a great week and a great party, thank you all for joining us." She looked at Bull sitting next to her, a content smile on his face. "I guess this is as good a time as any to make an announcement." He nodded approval and she continued. "We found out today that Kainani is going to have a baby brother to take care of next year."

Kainani yelped, sat straight up, jumped out of her chair, and ran around the table pumping her fists in the air.

Bull smiled. "He's gonna be a great beach boy, better than me."

Chris patted him on the back.

"Congratulations Bull, and Leilani." He thought he knew the answer but he wanted to hear it straight from a kanaka. "What's the Hawaiian word for this occasion?"

Bull thought for a quick moment, then answered decisively.

"Hana hou. One more."

Chris smiled and sat back in his chair full and content both physically and spiritually. Hana hou it was. What a Christmas this had turned out to be after all. He shook his head at the irony of it. A present gets undelivered and they end up becoming part of a great Hawaiian family.

Melissa looked at Leilani and winked, and Leilani winked back at her knowingly.

"Well," said Melissa. "This seems like as good a time as any for me to make an announcement as well. I was going to wait till we got home, but now is the time."

She smiled at Chris.

"Now's the time for what?" he asked, slightly dumbfounded.

"Hana hou," she said again, then handed him a flower.

His face turned blank, eyes wide and his jaw dropped a notch.

She continued:

"Hana hou Mr. Claussen, you're going to be a daddy."

His face turned blank. Boy or girl, or twins, it didn't matter and he didn't ask.

He sat straight up in his chair, reached over, and kissed her on the cheek, then jumped up and began to run around the table pumping his fists in the air, yelling at the top of his lungs:

"HANA HOU HOU HOU, AND A MERRY CHRISTMAS !!!

Kainani stopped him in his tracks, and pulled his shoulder down to her level so she could whisper in his ear and no one else could hear his real name:

"Mele Kalikimaka Santa."

And he nodded in agreement as the band started up for one final song; ukulele, steel guitar and bass notes drifting up into the star filled night, for it truly was a Merry Christmas, Hawaiian style.

All pau.

Made in the USA
Middletown, DE
28 December 2022

20583447R00085